Splash in

I took a deep breath. It alw... the world seemed at night. ... five feet in any direction with my flashlight on— beyond that, I had no idea what the darkness held.

Splash. Wait—had I really heard that? It sounded just feet away, in the river. Like someone stepping right in.

I breathed in again. *Calm down, Frank.*

THE HARDY BOYS

Undercover Brothers®

Available from Simon & Schuster

THE HARDY BOYS

Undercover Brothers

BOYS

FRANKLIN W. DIXON

#34 The Children of the Lost

BOOK ONE IN THE LOST MYSTERY TRILOGY

Aladdin

New York   London   Toronto   Sydney

❦

ALADDIN

An imprint of Simon & Schuster Children's Publishing Division
1230 Avenue of the Americas, New York, NY 10020
First Aladdin paperback edition May 2010
Copyright © 2009 by Simon & Schuster, Inc.
All rights reserved, including the right of reproduction in
whole or in part in any form.
ALADDIN is a trademark of Simon & Schuster, Inc., and related logo
is a registered trademark of Simon & Schuster, Inc.
THE HARDY BOYS MYSTERY STORIES is a trademark
of Simon & Schuster, Inc.
HARDY BOYS UNDERCOVER BROTHERS and related logo are
registered trademarks of Simon & Schuster, Inc.
For information about special discounts for bulk purchases,
please contact Simon & Schuster Special Sales at 1-866-506-1949 or
business@simonandschuster.com.
The Simon & Schuster Speakers Bureau can bring authors to your
live event. For more information or to book an event contact the
Simon & Schuster Speakers Bureau at 1-866-248-3049 or visit our website
at www.simonspeakers.com.
Designed by Sammy Yuen Jr.
The text of this book was set in Aldine 401 BT.
Manufactured in the United States of America/0310 OFF
10 9 8 7 6 5 4 3 2 1
Library of Congress Control Number 2010921648
ISBN 978-1-4424-0262-1
ISBN 978-1-4424-0263-8 (eBook)

TABLE OF CONTENTS

Prologue

Sunlight. Bright sunlight. The sun was overwhelming today, pushing through his closed eyes, forcing him awake. He reached out his hand, feeling damp ground, a few crumpled leaves beneath him. Hungry. He felt hungrier than he'd ever been, desire gnawing at his stomach. It had been . . . well . . . how long had it been since he'd last eaten?

He sat up, leaves clinging to his worn T-shirt and too-small jeans. He had been lying here in the woods for . . . a long time, hadn't he? Or had he? And before that . . .

He shakily got to his feet. He couldn't remember. He couldn't remember anything before these woods, this hunger.

His heart beat quickly in his chest. It was okay. It

would come back to him, right? The details of what he'd been doing . . . of who he was. Now he just had to get something to eat. He stumbled forward, toward a road he saw through the trees, an occasional car rushing by. Standing on the curb, he looked right and saw a small cluster of buildings.

Food. At the thought of it, his stomach let out an angry growl. He had to get something to eat, now. And there would be food in those buildings; he knew that much. Food that would quiet the growling, that would satisfy the hunger inside him.

He walked toward the buildings. The sun was nearly blinding, and it made him dizzy. A few times, he had to stop and close his eyes, wait for the sound of rushing blood to subside in his head. His body was weak, and it screamed to lie down again, to rest in the grass. But he forced himself forward.

As he reached the cluster of buildings, a few people walking along the streets or driving by openly stared at him. He could tell that something about his appearance troubled them, but he couldn't bring himself to care just then. Food was what he needed. Food was the only thing that mattered. If he could just eat, maybe everything else would fall into place.

Finally he stood in front of a low freestanding building. GENERAL STORE, the sign said. He pressed his face to the window and nearly cried out at the array of food that confronted him. Bright red tomatoes; cartons of milk; piles of cupcakes. Letting out a groan, he yanked the door open and darted inside, ignoring the cashier's calls as he ran to the shelves of vegetables. Without a word, he grabbed a ripe red tomato and shoved it in his mouth, gobbling it whole, red seeds and juice running down his chin. Then he picked up a green pepper and tore into its skin, crunching as he pulled off bright green pieces and shoved them into his mouth.

The cashier was yelling now, trying to get his attention, but he didn't care. He saw the dairy display to his left and grabbed a small carton of milk, pouring it down his throat. He saw a display of eggs and greedily grabbed at the first Styrofoam tray, opening the top to reveal twelve perfect white caps. As the cashier ran back to the front to make a call, he lifted an egg from the tray, shattered it in his hand, and let the runny insides flow into his mouth.

Nothing had ever tasted so good.

It was probably only minutes before the uniformed policeman showed up, but it felt like hours. In that time, he tore through an entire box of cookies, a bunch of bananas, and a bottle of ketchup. He was just beginning to feel satisfied—to feel like maybe he could concentrate on something other than eating—when a blue-sleeved hand reached out and grabbed his arm.

"Son," a voice said, equal parts concern and confusion, "what do you think you're doing?"

• • •

Twenty minutes later, he was in a new building, this one drab and gray and filled with uniformed people behind desks. The man who'd stopped him from eating sat him in a small room and settled on a chair a few feet away, looking at him like he was some sort of alien.

"Come on now, boy," he said for the third time now, "just tell me: What's your name?"

He cleared his throat, and his voice sounded new and foreign, even to him. "I don't know."

"How can you not know?" the redheaded officer asked gently, shaking his head. "Are you frightened? Trust me, boy, everything will be all right. We just need to call your parents."

Parents. He looked around the room, willing something to stir a memory in him. "I don't think I have parents."

The officer sighed deeply, and just then the door to the room opened, letting in a portly gray-haired man in a plaid button-down shirt and jeans.

"Hey there, Rich. Maybe you can help me get to the bottom of this. We picked up this boy in Flo's store, eating up his produce like he'd never seen food before. And look at the way he's dressed: like he just wandered out of the woods, right? Anyway, I keep asking him his name, trying to get some background, but the boy says he doesn't know. Says he doesn't know who he is!"

The portly man—Rich—looked up and met his eyes.

Rich's eyes were dark and hard, and they seemed to find something inside him that he couldn't find himself.

After a moment he spoke: "It's okay, Officer Donnelly. I know who the boy is, though I can't quite believe it myself." The detective shook his head. "Boy, if I'm not mistaken, your name is Justin Greer."

Justin Greer. Justin Greer. He repeated the syllables over and over in his head, but they meant nothing to him.

The detective sighed. "And Justin . . . you've been missing for more than eleven years."

A New York Minute

 Joe:

Here's something funny about the mole people who live in New York's subway system. You'd think they would be weird antisocial types, but they're not. Together, they've constructed this amazing underground city using just things they've found on the street and the electricity that runs the subway system. For example, this evening our host, Martha, made my brother, Frank, and me some excellent English-muffin pizzas for dinner—using a toaster oven she found in a trash can at the Times Square station.

Hands down, these were the best English-muffin pizzas I've ever had. Better than anything Frank's ever made me, with the benefit of a full kitchen and fresh ingredients from the grocery store.

Frank:

Frank here. I would use this opportunity, Joe, to dog your cooking, too—if you had ever cooked anything in your entire life.

Joe:

Touché, Frank. In any case, on a typical Friday night in May, my brother and I found ourselves in black pants and black hooded sweatshirts, soot rubbed all over our faces to cut down on glare, and crouched in an unused subway tunnel just south of City Hall station in Manhattan. We were on the lookout for M3, which is the code name for the secret money train that runs the whole system at night, collecting money from the MetroCard machines and ferrying it to an office in Brooklyn.

For the last month, large amounts of money had mysteriously gone missing off the money train. This was pretty weird, see, because the money train travels with an insane amount of security. Think about it: If you had to transfer money through the New York subway system—which never shuts down, by the way, so there are always passengers waiting in every station—wouldn't you be super careful about it? That's why M3 is a state-of-the-art vehicle. It's completely computerized—there's no way you're getting near that thing without twenty different security codes. Plus, it travels with at least two security guards. I'm just saying, if you're thinking of ripping off the New York subway to buy an Xbox or something, you might want to come up with an easier plan.

But the weird thing was, someone *was* ripping off the New York subway. Which meant someone *had* devised a way past all the security to get to that cold hard cash. And after two long weeks spending our nights in the dark tunnels below New York— while our mom and aunt Trudy thought we were house-sitting for a co-worker of my dad's—we'd fingered a likely culprit. Doug LaFayne, a middle-aged janitor at the City Hall station, was a secret computer genius. And Frank and I were pretty sure that after twenty years on the job, he'd devised a way to outsmart M3.

"Here it comes," whispered Frank, as the familiar whine and squeak of a train approaching at slow speed filled the tunnel. We both turned around: Sure enough, the shining silver, ultra-armored M3 was slowly pulling into the station.

I turned back to face the platform at the station. Sure enough, Doug LaFayne was loitering there, lazily pushing a mop around the tiled floor—but really, his attention was focused on a tiny controller device fastened to his wrist.

The train pulled into the station and stopped without making a sound—a rarity among New York subway trains, believe me. Frank and I had learned real fast that earplugs were a necessity in these tunnels. After a few seconds, a door in the middle of the train opened, and three people got out—the MTA officer in charge of emptying the machines, one guard to follow her to the machines, and one guard to stand at the entrance to the train.

Doug perked up, silently watching the officer and the guard walk through the turnstiles to the MetroCard machines. Sure enough, as soon as they were through the turnstiles, his right hand moved to the controller on his wrist. He began typing. Frank and I had discerned that he'd written a code to override the lock on a trapdoor that led from the bottom of M3 to the tracks below. By hacking into the train's security system and entering a simple four digit code, Doug had gained access to the money train.

The next part, though, was what was truly

amazing: Doug pushed a button on the controller, then made a big show of pushing around his mop, like he couldn't care less about the money train. Meanwhile, a tiny robot that Doug had installed in the space between the tracks and the platform sprang to life. It slid into the tiny space beneath the train, raised up, and entered the trapdoor in the M3's floor. Then it simply reached out a pair of electronic arms, grabbed a bin full of bags of change and bills, and pulled it out of the train and onto the tracks below. With the flick of another button, Doug commanded the robot to push the money into a barely visible space beneath the platform. Then the robot folded itself back up and settled into the same tiny space. Doug entered his four-digit code again, and the trapdoor locked back up. Easy peasy.

It was a pretty impressive operation, and in my opinion, it made Doug LaFayne an A-level Crazy Computer Genius. The thing about Crazy Computer Geniuses, though, is that once they get a taste of crime, they can turn very, very dangerous. That's why Frank and I were going to take down Doug tonight.

The MTA officer finished emptying the three machines, and the security guard trailed her back to the M3. The security guard who'd been guarding the door stepped aside, and together, all three boarded the train again. The door closed behind them, the air brakes huffed quietly, and the train pulled silently back into the tunnel. As Frank and I had been instructed, we sat perfectly still in the tunnel, waiting patiently. It was only a couple minutes before Doug glanced curiously after the train, looked around the empty station, and dropped his mop. Without a word, he ran over to the edge of the platform, knelt down, and swung himself down onto the tracks.

With the expert air of someone who'd done this a hundred times, he walked right over to his hiding place and pulled the plastic bin from its space beneath the platform. When he saw that the bin was filled to the brim with zippered bags of cash, he grinned. Opening one up, he pulled out a roll of twenty-dollar bills and let out a low whistle.

Funny thing about crooks. No matter how much money they've stolen, it's never enough.

I glanced at Frank and he nodded. This was our cue.

Scrambling from our hiding space, we launched ourselves over to the live track where Doug stood, careful to avoid the electrified third rail—the train's main source of power and a current so strong it could fry an adult in about thirty seconds. Doug startled the minute we started running, but he still wasn't prepared for the wrath of two well-trained ATAC agents.

"Hold it right there!" Frank shouted, and Doug grabbed the platform, trying to scramble up, but I grabbed his leg before he could.

"The gig's up, Doug," I said, gesturing toward the bin of money that he still clutched in his hands. "You've been ripping off the money train for weeks now. Well, you're pretty smart—but not smart enough to outwit us."

Just then, two uniformed NYPD officers came running down the stairs to the station. They'd been waiting outside for their cue to provide Frank and me with backup. I shoved Doug against the edge of the platform, sure that the cops would reach us before he'd be able to squirm away, but then something unexpected happened. Doug reached down to his controller and typed in a series of numbers.

The entrance the cops were heading toward wasn't a main entrance to the station. That meant that instead of entering via turnstile, the cops would have to scan their MetroCards and push their way through a heavy revolving gate. But as Frank and I watched, astonished, the cops scanned their cards and then shoved heavily into the gate—which didn't even budge.

"He locked it!" cried Frank, as stunned as I felt. "He must have hacked into the whole station's security system!"

The cops kept banging against the gate, futilely trying to make it move. "It's locked!" the younger officer yelled to us, shrugging helplessly. "We'll need to go to the main entrance!"

The main entrance to the station had turnstiles. Even if they were locked, the cops could jump over them. Thousands of fare dodgers over the years had risked the wrath of station agents to enter the subway this way. But the main entrance was a good two blocks from the entrance the cops had tried to use. That meant a delay of a minute or two—which could be just enough to derail our mission.

Seeing the cops outsmarted seemed to give Doug an extra jolt of energy. He bucked hard against me, pushing me back from the platform just enough to allow him to reach into his pocket. Before I could wonder what he was reaching for, I heard a sharp *Bzzzzt!* and Frank screamed. My brother *never* screams. I turned just in time to see my brother falling away from Doug, who triumphantly held out a Taser. He'd Tased my brother! And now Frank was falling . . . oh *no*. I sprang into action, grabbing my brother's limp, trembling body and shoving him back before he landed on the third rail.

Doug LaFayne laughed. "You think you can outsmart me?" He pushed the button on his Taser again, and it let out a sharp crackle of electricity. "After what I've managed here?"

I can't lie; I was *furious.* Normally Frank and I are pretty good at concealing our emotions during ATAC missions, but this guy had just *Tased* my *bro.* Making sure that Frank was positioned safely—not near the third rail—I lunged at Doug, easily knocking the Taser out of his hand. I shoved him back toward the platform, trying to force his head down onto the dirty platform surface. But he reared back with a surprising amount of strength, sharply elbowing me in the face.

Ouch! Okay, now I was really getting perturbed. At first, I have to admit, I was kind of impressed by Doug—I mean, not everyone can build a money-train-thieving robot. But now he just seemed like every other selfish, dim-witted crook we'd battled over the last few months. And he was going down. *Now.*

I swung hard, landing a solid punch to the back of his head. He groaned and pitched forward, but he quickly used the space he'd gained to swivel around and land a sharp blow to my stomach. I tried to dart away, as we'd been trained in basic self-defense, but he still got me pretty good, and I doubled over. He moved even closer, reeling back to punch me again, but then we heard a noise coming from the tunnel.

Screeeeeeee!

A train!

My heart pounded hard in my chest. *Frank!* I had enough time to get away, but more importantly, I had to get my brother off the tracks. Giving Doug a quick shove to give myself some space, I turned and knelt beside Frank, carefully lifting him under the shoulders and knees. I struggled under his weight to get to the platform and gently placed him on the waist-high lip, then placed my hands on the edge and carefully vaulted myself off the tracks. Safely on the platform, I grabbed Frank's semiconscious body and pushed him back from the tracks, well out of the way of the train and any departing passengers.

All of this transpired in about ten seconds. When I turned back, Doug was holding his bin full of money, frantically reaching down to pick up a few bags that had fallen onto the tracks. The train was approaching, but slowly—the subway trains often moved more slowly at night, I'd learned. It creaked around the corner of the tunnel, its bright headlights suddenly flooding the tracks with light.

I looked down at Doug, my heart beating hard. The cops still weren't here. And right now, the smartest thing for him to do would be to run *away* from me—through the dividers to the uptown tracks, then over and up onto that platform and out the exit. Once the oncoming train pulled into the station, it would block me, and I wouldn't be able to follow him. I could go aboveground, but there were so many exits, it would be nearly impossible to catch him that way.

I *couldn't* lose him.

Making a split-second decision, I leaped down from the platform, aiming right for Doug, tackling him onto the tracks. The train blared its horn, and my heart beat faster; I knew it was too late for a train going at that speed to stop. Pushing him down, I wrestled the bin from his hands, shoving it beneath the platform where it wouldn't impede the train. Then I grabbed his wrists and shoved them down. Climbing lengthwise on top of him, I tried to push both of our bodies as far down into the track bed as I could.

Doug screamed, trying to struggle away. "What are you trying to do, man?"

"Just *stay still*," I urged, making my voice low

and plain. "Unless you want to die. Stop struggling and stay exactly where you are."

The train was just feet away. I pushed my face down into the space of Doug's neck, smelling the dirt and fetid water of the track bed. The train ran over us swiftly. One minute there was the bright light of the headlights and lots of track space on either side; the next we were confined in a tiny, tomblike space between the bottom of the train, its wheels, and the track bed. Doug whimpered, and again I urged, "Don't move. It's over, Doug. You're caught." The train wheezed to a stop, and I heard the brakes engage. There were a few moments of silence before I heard footsteps scrambling down the steps and over the turnstiles.

"Freeze! NYPD! What's going on here?"

"We're under the train!" I screamed.

There was a pause. "*Under* the train?" the cop asked.

I laughed. I knew it would be a good while before the cops got us out from under this train, but it was worth it.

After all, the Hardy Boys *always* get their man.

Mission: Creepy

 Frank:

After the craziness of our subway mission, you'd think we would take a night off. Kick off our slippers. Settle in to watch a good DVD. But noooooooooo.

The next night, Joe decided that we had to do something that, for me, is way more difficult than battling criminal super-geniuses on a live track while a subway train approaches.

Joe:

Joe here. You'd think he was talking about performing open heart surgery, right? Well, I'll end the suspense. Here's what I set up for the night after our subway mission ended:

A double date.

Ooooooooooh!

Frank:

Sure, sure, laugh all you want, Joe. But the fact is, talking to girls can be . . . a little challenging for me. Things might start off okay—"Hi," "Hi," "How are you," "I'm fine"—but at some point I'll look up and she'll be *looking* at me, with big pretty eyes and a flirty smile, and the next thing I know . . . I just kind of . . .

Joe:

Clam up like a human Venus flytrap?

Frank:

Anyway. This is how we found ourselves at Pat's Putt-putt Emporium at about seven o'clock on Friday night. We were accompanied by two lovely ladies: Joe's date, Kirstie, a funny girl he knew from English class, and my date, Corinne, a very cute brunette girl who liked my jokes about alligators.

Joe:

Correction. Who *tolerated* his jokes about alligators.

Frank:

As I was saying. So far the date had been a little challenging for me. I mean, I have trouble making conversation with girls under normal circumstances, but Joe had decided to *really* torture me on this night: I was not allowed to bring up science, math, computers, logic . . .

Joe:

Basically, anything boring.

Frank:

Basically, anything I really like to talk about. Anyway, we were on our third or fourth hole, Kirstie was winning, and Corinne and I were chatting while Joe took his shot.

"So then," I told her, "the frog says, 'I guess you're feeling a little *snappy* today!' Get it? Snappy?"

Corinne laughed, but she seemed a little distracted. "Anyway, Frank," she said, "how was this week in school for you?"

This was a tough question, because normally I would say, "It was great—we dissected a worm in biology, and in my computer class, I wrote my very own spyware detection program!" But given that I had been strictly forbidden by my brother to mention such things, all I could choke out was,

"Um, it was okay—we had sloppy joes for lunch today."

Which was true. But boring. And besides, she knew—she ate in the cafeteria like me.

Pausing to tap her ball into the hole, she nodded slowly. "I see," she said. "Yes, they make a mean sloppy joe. But what . . . *else* did you do this week, Frank? Anything fun outside of school?"

I bit my lip. I was beginning to feel that familiar frozen, deer-in-the-headlights feeling I often get around ladies. If this were a date like any other, I would have told her about the robot I was attempting to build to clean Joe's room, or the fact that I had wired my alarm clock to my bedside lamp the day before so it would wake me up with natural, slowly building light. Then she would have looked incredibly bored and made some excuse about needing to get home to feed her cat. And I would have had to finish out the game as a lonely team of one.

Instead, I tried to think of what someone else might say. Someone with more . . . lady-friendly hobbies. "Oh yeah," I said, racking my brain. "I, uh . . . I made cupcakes."

Save! Everyone loves cupcakes, but especially girls.

Corinne looked surprised. "Cupcakes, huh? What did you make them out of?"

Shoot. "Oh, you know," I said with a shrug, moving forward to take another shot at my ball. "Stuff?"

I hit the ball with a little too much force, and it vaulted over the curb that surrounded the green and into a shallow pond.

"Nice one, Frank," Joe said with a grin, shaking his head. "I guess mini golf isn't your game."

I sighed. "Guess not." I went to retrieve my ball, and when I came back, my group had moved on to the next hole.

"We just gave you a six, Frank," Kirstie explained, giving me an apologetic look. "You were already at the stroke limit."

I nodded. "No problem."

After we'd taken our first strokes, Corinne caught up with me as I leaned against a huge wooden windmill.

"You want to know what *I* did this week?" she asked with an impish grin.

I nodded my head. "What? I would love to know."

Her eyes lit up. "I watched this special on television," she explained. "It was on one of the science channels? I watch them all the time. Anyway, this one was about global warming, and all the ways—"

I couldn't stop myself. "I saw that!" I cried. "The one with the French scientists and the computerized simulation—"

"Of what life would be like in Manhattan in fifty, one hundred, and two hundred years!" She grinned.

I nodded furiously. "Except that it wouldn't be there in two hundred years! It would be underwater!"

Corinne nodded in agreement. "Really, the whole thing made me want to live so much more greenly . . ."

"Well," I said, "I did see some problems with a few of their assumptions . . ."

Her eyes widened in recognition. "Like fuel standards staying the same in the U.S.! I just can't see—"

"*Frank!*" I turned around to see my brother trying to get my attention from across the green and looking a bit exasperated. Kirstie looked amused.

"Yes?" I asked innocently. But I had a feeling I knew what he was going to say. I had broken the rules—I had talked about science with Corinne. And yet she hadn't looked bored and tried to leave. What was *that* about?

"What are you guys talking about?" Kirstie asked, looking curiously at Corinne. "I haven't seen you guys get that animated since, well . . ."

"Ever?" Corinne laughed. "I'm sorry. I'm probably boring Frank. I'm just such a big dork; I love to talk about these science specials I watch on cable."

"No, no, *no!*" I insisted, turning away from my brother and looking into Corinne's eyes as sincerely as I could. "You weren't boring me at all! I love to talk about this stuff! In fact, I was just reading this book about global warming; it just came out . . ."

Corinne grinned. "Is it called *Earth in Peril*? Because I just checked that out of the library."

I shook my head in amazement. "That's exactly it," I replied. This was unreal. Not only was I *talking* to a *girl* . . . I was actually talking about a subject I loved and she seemed to love it just as much as I did! Was I dreaming?

"Psssst."

I startled. I had definitely just heard a noise, most likely human in origin . . . but Corinne was looking straight ahead, watching Kirstie putt, and her mouth was shut. Joe was leaning over, giving Kirstie some kind of instructions (typical Joe— she's beating him and he still has to put in his two cents), and Kirstie was biting her lip, using her club to figure out the exact direction in which she needed to aim. None of the people I was standing with had just spoken, and we were the only group in the immediate area. So who . . .

"Pssst," the voice came again. I jumped this time; it was coming from *inside* the windmill I was leaning against! "Agent Hardy, *look in the waterfall.* Repeat, look in the waterfall. Do you read me?"

I sighed. *Really?* Joe and I had just finished the subway mission—did ATAC really need us again so soon? And in the middle of this actually-really-fun date?

"Do you read me?" the voice hissed again, more insistent this time.

"I read you," I whispered, dropping my voice low enough so Corinne wouldn't hear. "I read you loud and clear."

Stepping forward, I announced, "Excuse me, I just need to . . . I'm going to run to the restroom for a second. Corinne, you can play for me." Without waiting for an answer, I darted off toward the main building—and a huge concrete waterfall splashing with blue-dyed water. Darting low to the ground, I crept over, then peered down into the blue pool at the base. I didn't see anything, so I reached my hand in and carefully felt alongside the rough concrete walls. Nothing there . . . nothing there . . .

I was practically leaning into the waterfall itself

when I felt it. A thin plastic package, about five inches square, duct-taped to the side of the pool. After checking to make sure that no one was watching me, I dislodged the tape and pulled out the plastic sleeve, carefully shaking it dry and shoving it into the waistband of my pants, where it would be hidden by my shirt.

I sighed. It was official: This had to be an assignment.

Well, no rest for the wicked.

Without hesitating, I walked back over to Joe, Kirstie, and Corinne, who were all laughing uproariously at what looked to be a disastrous putt by my brother.

"I'm sorry," I announced, trying to keep my voice as emotionless as possible. "It's just occurred to me that Joe and I haven't fed our cat today. I'm feeling rather guilty and think we should get home and feed her as soon as possible. I'm sorry to break up our fun."

"You are *unbelievable*, dude," Joe huffed, shaking his head and slamming his club down on the return table as we headed back into the parking lot and toward our car. "Our cat? *Our cat?* If you felt uncomfortable, couldn't you have come up with a better excuse?"

"Joe," I said in what I hoped was a calming tone, pulling the plastic-wrapped package out from under my shirt, "I—"

"It seemed like you were having such a good time!" Joe whined, pulling open the passenger side door of our car and dropping himself into the seat with a *thump*. "You didn't listen to me about the science thing, okay, but it seemed like you and Corinne were really getting along!"

I opened the driver side door and settled into the driver's seat. "We *were*," I insisted, holding up the plastic package. "I'm just as disappointed as you are, believe me. But I was instructed to go get this."

Joe turned to look at the package and his eyes widened. "Already?" he asked. It *was* unusual to be called on two missions so close together.

"Must be an emergency," I said.

Joe nodded. "Hurry up and play it," he suggested, grabbing our portable DVD player from the glove compartment and shoving it in my direction.

Taking care not to scratch the DVD, I cautiously opened up the player, placed the disk inside, and closed it—Joe sighing impatiently the whole time. When I finally pressed play, we both glued our eyes to the screen. What came up was a series of local news stories.

In the first, a young blond reporter gripped a microphone in front of what looked like a state park. "In Misty Falls today, a child is missing, and his parents are being questioned by local police. It seems that five-year-old Justin Greer disappeared from the tent the family was sleeping in last night . . ."

The picture jumped to another news report with a different, male reporter. "As I said, Cindy, police have reportedly found no evidence of foul play at the campsite where eight-year-old Kerry Bragg went missing last night. Her younger brother reported that she left the tent in the middle of the night to use the restroom, and apparently she never returned. Park rangers are suggesting that Kerry may have been the victim of a bear attack. Her parents . . ."

The screen jumped again, this time to yet another reporter, still in what seemed to be the same campground. "A chilling disappearance in Misty Falls State Park tonight, where five-year-old Sarah Finnegan disappeared from the campsite where she and her older sister were sleeping outside . . ."

Again, to yet another reporter: ". . . seven-year-old Luke Wesson disappeared from the car where he slept with his parents . . ."

Another reporter, another story: ". . . four-year-old Alice disappeared, only a quarter mile from the campsite, while on a hike with her brother . . ."

The screen kept jumping and showing new footage, all of which seemed to be from the same state park. But then, the authoritative voice of our ATAC contact drowned out the reporting.

"Eight children disappeared in all, over the course of twelve years, all taken from their campsites along the Eagle River in Misty Falls, Idaho. Little evidence was found, and with the input of local park rangers and nature experts, all eight disappearances had been dismissed as animal attacks—most likely, bear."

"She said *had*," Joe observed.

"Intriguing," I agreed. "That would imply that it's changed."

The news reports faded, and the screen suddenly was filled with the image of a teenage boy, maybe fifteen or sixteen, wearing a hospital gown and looking forlornly into the camera. "The last thing I remember is waking up in the woods outside town," he said, his voice uncertain, as though he already knew this was the wrong answer. "That was yesterday. I don't remember where I was before that or where I came from. I don't know who my parents are."

A second voice sounded then from behind

the camera: "You don't know? Or you don't remember?"

The boy coughed, looking uncomfortable. He glanced down at his lap, then back at the camera, a challenging look in his eyes. "They tell me," he said, "that my name is Justin Greer."

I turned to Joe. "Justin Greer!" I said. "That was the first kid who disappeared."

Joe looked perplexed. "So that was what . . . twelve years ago? And he's just reappearing now?"

The smooth voice of our ATAC contact cut off our conversation. *"Two days ago, a teenage boy stumbled into downtown Misty Falls, claiming to have no idea who he was. A local police detective who worked the original disappearance case identified him as Justin Greer, and the boy's parents have arrived and identified the boy. Justin, however, has no memory of the Greers, nor any memory of the past twelve years. His reappearance is understandably making the police re-evaluate their findings on all eight disappearances. If Justin Greer wasn't attacked by a bear but is still alive . . . what happened to him? And what does it mean for the other missing children?"*

I let out a deep breath. "Whoa."

Our contact went on: *"The detective who identified Justin Greer has asked for an ATAC investigation. Because the disappearances were highly publicized in the* area and have led to declined tourism, there's been a lot of finger-pointing and controversy, which led the detective to believe an undercover investigation would be most beneficial. Your mission is to travel to Misty Falls, set up a campsite in the park, and investigate both what happens there and whatever memories might be coaxed out of Justin—if he is, indeed, Justin."

The screen went blank. I turned to Joe, who looked less than enthusiastic. "Well?" I asked.

Joe shivered. "It gives me the creeps," he replied. "Bear, my eye—someone or something is taking those kids."

I sighed patiently. "Now, Joe, we don't know that. Bears are known to—"

But Joe held up his hand to stop me. "Whatever, whatever," he said, "we'll have plenty of time for this argument on the plane. For now, we'd better come up with a heckuvan excuse for Mom and Aunt Trudy. Because it looks like we're leaving on an unexpected camping trip tomorrow."

Tragedy in Misty Falls

A s it turned out, coming up with a cover story for Mom and Aunt Trudy wasn't as hard as I'd feared. Dad knows all about our ATAC missions, so he helped us convince them that we were taking two places that had opened up at the last minute for a "personal development camping trip" offered by the National Honor Society. Mom and Aunt Trudy were skeptical, but when Dad insisted that we'd be *right* nearby (which is not *technically* a lie, since it depends on your definition of "nearby") and that it would "really look great on college applications," they were sold.

And so my brother and I found ourselves climbing off a tiny four-seater plane just a few miles out of Misty Falls, Idaho.

"It's beautiful here," I observed, taking in the wide blue sky, the distant mountains, and the acres and acres of unspoiled forest land.

"Big Sky Country," Frank agreed, looking around. "That's what they call it, and I can see why."

I nodded. "It seems like *everything* is bigger here than on the east coast—the sky, the mountains, even the trees."

That's when I looked down and saw a tall, portly middle-aged guy wearing a cowboy hat watching us. He was smiling, but it didn't look like a "Welcome to Idaho!" smile so much as a "You east coast types are *heee*-larious!" smile.

"Hello," I said cheerfully, walking down the steps to the tarmac and holding out my hand. "I'm Joe Hardy and this is my brother, Frank. You must be Detective Cole?"

He nodded, taking off his cowboy hat and smiling a warm, genuine smile. "Call me Rich," he said, stepping aside to gesture to a blue-and-white Misty Falls police car. "I'm so glad y'all are here. I hope with your help, we might finally be able to get some answers for these parents."

We both nodded. "We'd really love to help you

do that," Frank agreed. "They all deserve some closure. ATAC told us they would send our gear to you?"

Rich nodded. "It's all waiting for you at the station," he said. "In fact, let's head there now. I'd like to fill you two in on the story as it stands right now."

Frank and I tossed our small knapsacks of essentials into the trunk and slipped into the car for the ride to town. It only took forty-five minutes, but we must have gone fifty miles down the highway easily, before turning off at a stoplight where a tiny sign promised MISTY FALLS BUSINESS DISTRICT, LEFT."

"Was that the closest airport?" I asked Rich. "We'd hate to have made you drive out of your way."

Rich laughed—a deep, throaty laugh. "Now I know y'all are city folk," he said. "For us westerners, fifty miles is just a hop, skip, and jump down the road."

We drove down the street we'd turned onto, which looked to be Misty Falls's main street—blink and you'd miss it! A modest general store stood alongside a hardware store, a tiny diner-type place called Jack's, and the police station.

"Wow," I said. "This is . . . homey."

Rich chuckled. "It ain't New York City, that's for sure."

Frank was looking around the town center with his eyebrows furrowed. "You guys don't have a post office, even? I thought every town had a post office."

Rich laughed again. "Oh, you city kids. We have a P.O.—Flo runs it out of the general store. In fact, they can't seem to find a driver who wants to cover a fifty-square-mile territory, so everybody comes into Flo's a couple times a week to pick up their mail. Nobody's missing much, far as I can tell."

He'd pulled into a tiny parking lot that hugged the side of the old brick police station. Once he parked, we all stepped out into the bright sunlight, and then Rich ushered us inside.

"Hey there, Rich!" a young uniformed cop with a red buzz cut and lots of freckles called as we walked inside.

"Hey there, Kurt," Rich replied, smiling as he led us down the hall toward an unmarked door. "I'm gonna have a little talk with these young students, Frank and Joe. They're down from the university, wanting to ask me some questions about a paper they're writing on those poor eight kids."

Kurt's eyes widened in recognition. "Oh, I see," he said, nodding slowly. "You boys are wasting your time, y'know—I don't know what happened to that poor boy at the hospital, but those kids were attacked by bears, sure as I'm sittin' here."

I looked back at him, not sure what to say. *Thanks? I think you're not looking at this objectively?* But before I could say anything, Rich took my arm and pulled me into a small interview room. Once Frank and I were inside, he shut the door firmly behind me.

"That's a pretty common opinion around here, I think you'll find," Rich told us, giving us a warning look. "People don't want to believe a horrendous crime like the abduction of eight children could have happened in their town. It's much easier to believe it was an accident—unfortunate but natural."

Frank looked confused. "But after everything—it's happened so many times now—don't they want the criminal caught, if there is one? Aren't they worried about the safety of their children?"

Rich sighed. "Well, it's like this. Most of the children who have disappeared so far have been from outside—tourists, summer vacationers." He paused. "As tough as it is to understand, I think folks in town think they know better than those tourists. You know, we know the land here—and if you know what you're doing, you won't get in trouble."

I nodded. "And the families who lost children didn't know what they were doing?"

Rich took off his hat and ran a hand through his hair. "I don't want to make the locals sound heartless," he said. "Everyone here felt terrible for those poor folks. Nobody wants to see a parent lose a child," he added. "I think you'll find, though—given a choice between worrying about something and not worrying, people will always choose the option that allows them to not worry. In this case, believing those were bear attacks makes the townsfolk feel secure. It allows them to sleep at night."

I glanced at my brother and nodded. "That makes sense," I said.

Rich nodded slowly, then looked off into the distance, seeming to deflate a little. "As for me, I sleep terribly at night, especially lately." He paused and looked me right in the eye. "Because I think I may have helped cover up the biggest crime around here in decades."

Over the course of a couple hours, Rich told us everything we needed to know about the Misty Falls Lost, as the media had crowned the missing eight children. Eight kids, all between the ages of four and eight, all missing from the same park within a span of twelve years. Very little evidence found at each campsite, no footprints, no finger-prints, no DNA. For a long time, no evidence of the children was found . . . until five years ago. Park rangers were removing a sick grizzly bear from the park, and in the cave where it had been hibernating, they found bones that, after DNA testing, turned out to belong to one of the little girls who disappeared. It was a heartbreaking discovery—especially for the parents who'd held out hope of finding their child alive someday—but it also gave credence to the "it was just a bear" theory. If this poor little girl had been the victim of a bear attack, chances were the others had, too.

As the disappearances continued, though, the story took on a life of its own. Gradually, the tone of the news coverage became less, "Another tragedy in Misty Falls" and more, "What the heck is going on?" Rumors and legends began circling about the disappearances. A ghost story sprang up about a hiker who'd gotten dangerously lost in the park and ended up starving to death. He—local kids referred to him as "Nathan," though whether an actual Nathan existed was never verified—was claimed to have taken the children as revenge for his own miserable death. Rich thought the story came from an actual piece of evidence in the case; police had photographed the word "lost" written in the dirt with a stick at one of the missing children's campsites, and several eyewitnesses claimed that the word was scrawled in the dirt at the other abduction sites, too. Those who spread the ghost story claimed that Nathan was lamenting his own fate with the word scrawled in the mud. If he had never become lost, he would have lived—and now, to share his misery, he was making these poor children "lost," as well.

"It's total bunk," Rich told us, not mincing words. "There was never a body found of any lost hiker fitting Nathan's description. This is just kids telling stories—people trying to make sense of the unexplainable."

Frank nodded slowly. He's a logical guy, so of course that made sense to him. I, on the other hand, had to admit that my stomach felt a little funny at the thought of the park where we were planning to spend the next seven nights being haunted.

"Can you tell us more about Justin?" Frank asked.

"Of course," said Rich. "He's the reason you're here, really. Before he showed up, it was just accepted that all of these poor kids became some nasty animal's dinner. But now that Justin's returned—well, it puts a whole new face on the abductions."

"You said *abductions*," I observed, raising an eyebrow. "Not disappearances."

Rich sighed. "Well, boys, if you want to know the truth, maybe I never believed they were 'disappearances.' To me, it seemed clear that these children were being *taken*. To where and for what purpose, I don't know. But . . ." He paused, his eyes wet with emotion. "Boys, the last little girl we lost, someone cut a flap in the tent where she was sleeping and just pulled her out like a loaf of bread." He sighed, wiping at his eyes. "Does that sound like a bear? Or a mountain lion? Or anything besides the most dangerous animal in the forest—man?"

Frank frowned and nodded. "Well, it definitely sounds like there's a lot to be explained."

Rich nodded, looking away. After a moment, he seemed to collect himself and turned back to us. "Anyway," he said, "Justin. I can't imagine where he's been or what he's seen. If he could just *tell* us, we'd be so much closer to understanding what really happened." He sighed. "But he doesn't remember. He doesn't remember where he's been, what his name is—he doesn't remember anything."

I nodded slowly. "Can you tell us—what have his doctors said about his memory loss? Is there a reason for it? Do they think it's permanent?"

Rich looked thoughtful, then suddenly sprang up from the desk he'd been sitting on. "I can do better than tell you," he said. "I can take you to the hospital. Come on, boys—it's time for you to meet Justin Greer."

Mercy Hospital was located about ten minutes outside the center of Misty Falls. It was a big compound off a smaller state highway, huge and strangely incongruous in the middle of the prairie.

"This is the best hospital around for a hundred miles," Rich explained, "and the best-kept secret. It's staffed with top doctors and specialists, and when necessary, they bring in experts from the university hospital about two hours away."

Outside, the buildings looked rustic—split beams, rough wood, lots of big glass windows. But inside, I was almost dismayed to find that it looked (and smelled) just like any other hospital. Clean, tiled—antiseptic. All of the homey charm of the exterior was lost.

Rich took us briskly up to the third floor. "Psych ward," he explained. "That's where they're keeping Justin for now, since most of his problems are mental, not physical."

I nodded. "And how's he taking to his care here?"

Rich looked thoughtful. "He's very polite," he said after a moment. Right then, the elevator doors opened and he ushered us out. "Well, you'll see."

Rich led us down the main corridor to a smaller corridor, and then three doors down to a large corner room. "Justin?" he called inside, sounding almost timid. "It's me, Detective Richard Cole. I've brought some friends of mine to meet you."

Frank and I hesitantly entered the room behind Rich. I can't speak for my brother, but I wasn't sure what we'd find lying there in that hospital bed. A wild child? A foundling? But what confronted us when we looked up was a perfectly normal looking, almost bored teenage boy. His black hair was a little long and was pushed back from his face and behind his ears. He did, when I looked hard at his features, bear more than a passing resemblance to the young boy whose pictures had appeared on the news when Justin Greer disappeared. Otherwise, though, he looked like any kid we might have run across at Bayport High.

Justin took us in quietly, and it was a few seconds before he seemed to realize he was supposed to say something. "Hello," he said finally. "I'm . . . they tell me I'm Justin."

Frank stepped forward. "Nice to meet you, Justin," he said, holding out his hand to be shaken.

"I'm Frank, and this is my brother, Joe. We're students down from the university, interested in your case."

If Justin understood why Frank was holding out his hand, he made no indication of it. Instead, he sniffed the air.

"Dinner," he said. "I smell chicken. It must be coming from down the hall."

I sniffed, but I couldn't detect any hint of dinner smells in the air. Still, within thirty seconds or so, I heard it. The dinner cart rattled in the hall, and soon, a nurse in blue scrubs appeared in the doorway.

"Good evening, Justin," she said with a smile, hoisting a covered plate off the cart. "I have some baked chicken for you."

"Thank you very much," said Justin.

She placed the plate on a tray in front of him and raised the cover. Without even waiting for her to get the cover all the way off, Justin dug in. Even stranger, he didn't bother to unwrap the silverware that was bunched in a napkin at the side of his plate. He dug in with his fingers, grabbing the chicken and tearing the flesh off the bone with his teeth. Then he dropped that and scooped up a clump of mashed potatoes and gravy with two arched fingers. I glanced at Detective Cole. He raised an eyebrow and gave a little shrug like, *Well, what can you do?*

After a few minutes, Justin seemed to slow down and looked apologetically up at us. "I'm sorry," he said. "I know it's rude to eat in front of others. It's just that I'm very hungry."

Frank looked surprised. "No, it's—it's totally fine, Justin. Go ahead."

Justin scooped up a couple green beans with his hand and ate them. "I suppose you're wondering," he said, "what I remember."

"We're curious, yes," I spoke up.

Justin turned to look at me head-on. His dark eyes were completely serious; there was no element of irony or doubt in his expression at all. "I don't remember anything," he said slowly.

Then he picked up his cup of pudding and began licking out the leftovers.

Just then, a young, pretty brunette with curly hair pulled back in a ponytail walked in. She wore a red-and-white-striped outfit—the outfit of the candy-striper volunteers. At first, she seemed not to notice Frank or me, and she headed right for Justin.

"Good evening, Justin!" she said cheerfully. "I'm glad to see you're eating well; you still have a good appetite."

Justin eyed her quietly. "Thank you," he said formally, and then pushed his empty plate away.

The girl moved to take his tray, but then suddenly she seemed to realize that there were others in the room. She turned to face Frank and me with a startled expression. "Oh!" she cried.

Rich moved forward. "Good evening, Chloe. We didn't mean to startle you."

"Oh," Chloe said with an awkward shrug, "no worries. You didn't." It was pretty clear that we had, though. She turned to take in me, and then Frank. Her eyes lingered for a few seconds as she hurriedly adjusted her jumper. Frank just kept looking at her, too . . . like she was some exotic animal we'd happened upon.

"Hi, Chloe," I said pointedly, seeing that my brother was not going to introduce us. "I'm Joe, and this is my brother, Frank."

"They're students from the university," Justin added, his hands neatly folded under his tray. "They've come to research a paper on me."

Chloe finally tore her eyes away from Frank, smiling at Justin. "Is that right? I guess you're quite the celebrity."

Justin just stared at her blankly.

"Do you know what that means, Justin?" Rich asked after a moment. "To be a celebrity?"

Justin shook his head neatly, staring at his empty tray. "I do not."

Chloe sighed, and her eyes welled with what seemed to be sympathetic tears. "Don't worry, Justin," she said, "you'll remember everything soon."

She grabbed his tray, and Rich caught my eye and nodded, pointing toward the door. "We'll be back, Justin. I just want to introduce these boys to your doctors," he explained.

A few minutes later, we were back in the hall, headed for the nurses' station.

"That was odd," Frank observed, understated as always.

"He's so *polite*," I added. "But there's something— *wild* about him. Eating with his hands, not seeming to know how to talk to people."

Rich nodded. "That's not the half of it," he told us in a low voice. "Wherever or whatever he comes from, Justin isn't used to being confined. In his first couple nights here, he slipped past the doctors and nurses several times. Once, they found him in the laundry room, asleep in a pile of clean linens. And one time a security guard found him outside—just sitting perfectly still in an azalea bush. *Watching* him."

I couldn't help it—I whistled. "Whoa," I said.

"I'm sure he's a nice kid, but . . . that is some creepy stuff."

"It's not really that strange," Frank insisted logically. "If he really has been living outside . . ."

Detective Cole shrugged. "I think it's safe to say, wherever he's been for the last twelve years, it hasn't been your typical upbringing in the suburbs." He glanced up, spotting a tall gray-haired man with a short beard who was wearing a pair of green scrubs. "Aha! Doctor Hubert—just who I wanted to see."

The doctor looked up, his expression warming when he saw the detective. "Rich. What brings you here today? I thought the interrogations were done for now."

Rich nodded. "They are. I just wanted to bring by these two boys and introduce you. This is Frank and Joe, students from the university who are doing a paper on our Misty Falls Lost."

Was it just me, or did some of the warmth drain from Dr. Hubert's face? "Isn't that interesting?" He looked up suddenly, seeming to recognize a face behind us. "Doctor Carrini! Why don't you come meet these boys." He turned back to us, explaining, "Dr. Carrini is a memory expert down from the university as well—he's consulting on Justin's case."

We turned to welcome a medium-height dark-haired man in about his forties. He had dark, deep-set eyes, and he seemed to look at Frank and me with some degree of suspicion—or maybe that was just his natural expression. "Hello," he said in a calm, low voice, holding out his hand for me to shake. "I'm Douglas Carrini. Pleased to meet you."

Frank and I said hellos and shook his hand, then Frank spoke. "Can you—either of you, Dr. Hubert or Dr. Carrini—tell us what you know about Justin's condition?"

Dr. Hubert spoke first. "Well, physically he's fine—a bit dehydrated when he was first admitted, but we've taken care of that now. Other than that, nothing is wrong with him at all. No head trauma, brain damage—that sort of thing." He glanced at Dr. Carrini, who nodded.

"Memory-wise," Dr. Carrini told us, "he is, as you know, completely lost. He has no memory of any part of his life before Thursday—not his name, not where he lives, not his age, nothing."

I nodded. "And his parents have come to see him, right?" I asked. "Has he recognized them?"

Dr. Carrini looked dismayed. "Not at all," he said simply.

"Is that unusual?" Frank asked.

Dr. Carrini shrugged. "It's not unheard of. I think it's safe to say that Justin is suffering from some sort of psychological trauma, either brought on by a recent event or by the cumulative effect of whatever he's experienced over the last twelve years. It's not unusual for the brain to shut down in such cases—it's a form of self-protection."

I nodded. "So he will, eventually, get his memory back?"

"I hope so," Dr. Carrini replied. "It does concern me somewhat that Justin isn't responding to memory triggers, like his parents' arrival or family photographs and home movies. I'm looking for physical causes now but not finding anything."

I glanced at Frank. *Huh.* So Justin's situation *was* unusual.

"Are his parents coming back tonight?" Frank asked, seeming to read my thoughts. "Could we meet them?"

Dr. Carrini tilted his head to the side. "As it happens, Justin's mother just returned from the cafeteria. She's in his room now. Come, I'll bring her out and introduce you."

Detective Cole, Frank, and I all followed Dr. Carrini back down to Justin's room. Dr. Hubert gave us a little wave as he continued on his rounds. Just before we reached Justin's room, Dr. Carrini signaled to us to wait in the hallway while he disappeared inside. A few seconds later, he returned, followed by a short, plump red-haired woman with a kind face, wearing a sweater embroidered with apples.

"Hello," she said quietly, looking from Frank to me. "Oh, hello, detective. I'm Edie Greer."

Frank and I introduced ourselves, and Frank said, "This must be a very complicated time for you."

She nodded, her eyes watering. "It's a lot of conflicting emotions," she admitted. "Of course, we're so thrilled to find Justin *alive*, after all these years!" She looked gratefully at Rich, and he smiled.

"But . . . ," she went on, "it *has* been difficult, the last couple days. I can't tell you what it feels like to see a child . . . *your* child . . . just look through you like he doesn't know you from a stranger! I mean, I used to bathe Justin and feed him. He was afraid of the dark when he was little, so I would sing him to sleep. . . ." Her voice cracked, and her face seemed to melt into a sob. She brought up her hands, fiercely wiping her eyes. She took a deep breath, clearly struggling to control herself.

"Of course," she said finally, "he'll get better. He *will* remember me, I know."

Dr. Carrini nodded, looking thoughtful. "We certainly hope so."

I tried to catch Frank's eye to get his reaction to that. It seemed an odd thing to say to a suffering mother—but maybe Dr. Carrini was just being logical, scientific? Frank would certainly understand *that*.

But my brother's eyes were already following something down the hall. I glanced back and saw the candy striper, Chloe, approaching with a tall, broad salt-and-pepper-haired man in a flannel shirt.

Edie seemed to sigh—or maybe I was just imagining that? Dr. Carrini looked up and smiled, gesturing back to Frank and me. "Here's someone else for you boys to meet," he announced. "This is Jacob Greer—Justin's dad."

Of course. As soon as Dr. Carrini said it, I could see the family resemblance. Justin and Jacob shared the same dark hair, the same curious expression.

"Hello," I said, holding out my hand. "I'm Joe, and this is my brother, Frank. We're writing a paper on the so-called Misty Falls Lost. We're so sorry to bother you at this difficult time. Your wife was just explaining to us how hard these last few days have been."

Jacob looked at me like I had three heads, and for a moment I wondered if I'd said something horribly inappropriate. But then he shrugged and the moment seemed to pass. "You oughta know that Edie here is my ex-wife, I guess," he said gruffly. "We split up not long after Justin was gone. That's for starters."

I could feel my face turning red. *Oops.* Frank and I had worked on missing child cases before, and we knew that it wasn't unusual for couples to split up after losing a child. No matter how much they loved each other, sometimes the pain was too great.

"Then," Jacob added, fiddling with his suspenders, "you should know that I'm not convinced that kid in there is my boy. He could be, or he couldn't. He doesn't recognize me, and I'm not so sure about him."

Rich cleared his throat. "Jacob has requested that we do a DNA test," he said in a low voice. "The results should be back very soon."

Edie nodded a little forcefully. "That's right. We should know tomorrow or the next day. And *then*—once we're all sure that this is really our baby—then Justin can focus on remembering our family, and Jacob will start to accept him, I know it." She wiped away a tear that had escaped.

Jacob made a funny sound—somewhere between a snort and a throat-clearing. "And if that's our boy, we'll live happily ever after?" He shook his head, then turned to face me. "Let me tell you something, boy. These child abduction cases—they never end happily. Even if that is my son, he's been gone for twelve years now. I dunno what he's been through. But he's been someone else's longer'n he was mine."

I wanted more than anything to try to catch my brother's eye, but Jacob's eyes were boring into mine, daring me to look away. I held his gaze.

"Even if that *is* our son," Jacob added, gesturing vaguely to the boy in the hospital room, "odds are, he ain't never going to be the same. And the sooner we accept that, the better off we'll all be."

Edie let out a wail. Rich moved forward quickly, folding her into a hug. She whimpered into his shoulder, and he patted her back. "Now, Edie," he said gently, shooting an accusatory look at Jacob. "Now, Edie."

Jacob glanced at his sobbing wife. An expression passed quickly over his eyes—something like regret, or sadness—but it was gone before I could truly identify it. Then he shook his head and walked right past Edie into the hospital room.

Finally I caught my brother's eye. He looked just as stunned as I felt.

Camping Out

Not long after our introduction to Jacob Greer, Rich seemed to think it was a good time to bring us out to our new campgrounds at Misty Falls State Park. We left the hospital with little protest, saying a quick good-bye to Justin and his parents. Chloe, the candy striper, saw us on our way out and said it was nice to meet us and she hoped she'd see us again.

Joe gave me kind of a pointed look right then, but I'm not sure why.

The drive out to the state park only took about ten minutes, but by the time we pulled into the driveway, we hadn't seen a house or any sign of civilization for miles. Rich paused at the ranger station to say hello to the young lady working and to explain that he was dropping off some students (us) to camp. Then he continued on into the park.

So far, every bit of Idaho we'd seen had been beautiful, and the park was no exception. Huge pine and juniper trees stretched toward the sky, and a deep blue river cut through the forest before a string of purple mountains. I took in a calming breath, enjoying the clean country air.

"You'll be camping on the banks of the Eagle River," Rich explained to us, "which is where all of the disappearances took place, within a range of about five square miles."

"Really?" asked Joe, a hint of nervousness in his voice. I don't know if Rich heard it, though. I may have heard it only because he was my brother.

Rich nodded. "And I should warn you boys—there are most definitely bears living in this area. So be careful. Put all your food in airtight containers away from the tent."

Joe took a deep breath.

"We know," I assured Rich. "Don't worry about us—we've had extensive wilderness training as part of ATAC."

Rich pulled to a stop in a small parking lot

where a well-marked path disappeared into the woods. "I sure hope I did the right thing bringing you boys here."

We unloaded our gear, which ATAC had shipped to the police station. Then Rich walked us down the path into the woods. We walked for what seemed like ten miles but was probably only one or two, max. Jet lag and the long day were starting to catch up with me, though—I felt sleepy already.

"Here we are," Rich announced as we arrived at a little clearing on the banks of a shallow, rocky river. "Home sweet home."

Joe and I took in the site. Woods on three sides, the river and an exquisite view of the mountains on the fourth. If I hadn't known eight children had mysteriously disappeared nearby, I would have thought it the ideal vacation spot.

"It seems quiet," Joe observed, looking around. "Are there always so few campers here?"

Rich looked troubled. "Lately, yes," he said. "The rumors about the abductions are catching up with us."

There was silence for a moment, but finally I said, "Well. We sure do appreciate you bringing us out here, Rich, and taking your whole afternoon to get us situated. We'll be in touch soon."

Rich nodded. "You need any help setting up camp?"

Joe shook his head. "We'll be fine. But thanks."

Rich nodded again, then touched the brim of his cowboy hat in a silent good-bye. As we watched, he disappeared back into the woods.

Once I was fairly sure he was out of earshot, I turned to my brother. "So what do you think?" I asked.

Joe's eyes widened. "I'm pretty freaked, how 'bout you?"

I sighed. "No," I said, shaking my head. "About Justin? The case? What are your first impressions?"

Joe looked around at the trees, still uncomfortable. "My first impression is, this is really freaky," he replied. When I sighed again, he continued. "Look—I really don't know yet what's going on with Justin. On the one hand, there's no way he could have survived on his own in the wilderness for so long, but on the other, he doesn't seem like a kid who was raised by normal, loving parents."

I nodded. "He's a little wild."

"Yeah," Joe agreed. "And I think what freaks me out about this case is that nothing about it makes sense. Some of the clues seem to lead in one direction, but there are just as many leading in the other. Were the kids kidnapped? Were they killed by a man? Were they killed by a bear? Were they attacked by a ghost?"

I let out a sharp laugh. "A *ghost*? Come on, Joe. I think we can eliminate that one."

"*Can* we?" asked Joe, giving me a challenging look. "Part of me thinks a ghost is the only thing weird enough to really make sense here." He paused. "Kids disappearing in the middle of the night? Nobody ever hears anything, and there's never any evidence? Do you really think a human being could be so quiet and leave nothing behind?"

I took a deep breath. "It *is* hard to believe, Joe, but yes, I believe it because I have to," I replied. "Or, it might really have been a bear. Or, some of those kids might have wandered off on their own. It's unlikely, but those are the only explanations that make *sense*."

Joe shook his head. "They don't make sense at all! To me, the story about Nathan and his ghost makes a lot more sense."

I shook my head. "You don't mean that."

"I do," Joe insisted. "Frank, didn't you ever see *The Blair Witch Project*?"

I scoffed. *"No,"* I replied. "And it looks silly. Besides, Joe, even *you* must realize that story was fictional."

Joe just shook his head, looking down at the ground. "I'm going to have trouble falling asleep tonight," he muttered. "That's all I'm saying."

As it turned out, we decided to sleep in shifts. One of us would sleep while the other kept guard, watching and waiting to see if anything suspicious took place. Nobody except Rich and the park rangers knew we were camping in the park—at least, as far as we knew—so we didn't expect any trouble. Still, just being around and getting a sense of what went on in the park at night—what animals were present, that kind of thing—would help us figure out this case.

Joe took the first shift, then woke me up at midnight.

"Anything happen?" I asked curiously as I sat up in my sleeping bag, rubbing my eyes.

Joe shrugged. "Absolutely nothing," he replied with a yawn. "And believe me, no one's more shocked than I am." He settled down in his sleeping bag and adjusted his pillow while I pulled myself into a sitting position and flicked on my flashlight. Pulling out a recent copy of *Science* magazine, I soon got lost in an article about hydroponics.

"Joe," I said after about fifteen minutes of listening to him toss and turn and sigh. "Go to sleep. Really. It will be all right."

Joe didn't answer—he just sighed deeply. "This really doesn't frighten you at all?" he asked.

I shrugged. "It's just a quiet night in the Idaho wilderness," I replied. "Really, I'm enjoying how quiet it is. Now get some sleep."

I turned my focus back to my article, and a few minutes later, Joe's breathing turned slow and rhythmic. I smiled to myself. Good—he'd managed to calm down. I knew my brother would be a bear in his own right if he didn't get any sleep tonight.

I'd read through almost my whole magazine when I began to shift uncomfortably, and I cast my eyes toward the zipped opening of the tent. Mother Nature was calling me—but I wasn't so hot to answer. I was nice and warm where I was, sitting cross-legged with my sleeping bag and pillow wrapped around me. Besides . . . the wind had picked up, and it was probably cold out there. Every so often I heard a rumble in the distance. And the spot Joe and I had chosen for our latrine was a good forty yards from the tent.

Still. I sighed and slowly got to my feet. When you have to go, you have to go, and this couldn't wait. I gently smoothed my sleeping bag and pillow and grasped my big yellow flashlight. *All right—guess I'm going outside.*

I carefully unzipped the tent and stepped out. Outside, it seemed a million times darker than it had in the tent, and it took a few minutes for my eyes to adjust to the darkness and make out the river, the trees, and the remains of our fire.

I took a deep breath. It always amazed me how vast the world seemed at night. I could make out maybe five feet in any direction with my flashlight on— beyond that, I had no idea what the darkness held.

Splash. Wait—had I really heard that? It sounded just feet away, in the river. Like someone stepping right in.

I breathed in again. *Calm down, Frank.* I was getting just as bad as Joe. Just because I heard a splash in the night didn't mean it was a person—it could just as easily be a frog, a turtle, a fish. I was in nature's territory now, not my own. We were probably surrounded by hundreds of animals I'd never seen before, or ever would again.

Rrrrrumble. Thunder, and it sounded close. I'd better do my business and get back inside before I got soaked.

I picked my way through the darkness to the latrine area in the woods that Joe and I had chosen. As quickly as I could, I relieved myself and turned back to face the tent. Just for a moment, I shut off the flashlight to see if I could get my bearings and understand where the river was in relation to where I stood. A few seconds later, the whole area was lit up by a bolt of lightning—and my heart stopped.

Right there.

Right *there*!

Just a few feet to my left.

I'd spotted a bulky, dark, black-clothed figure—indisputably human, with an arm raised as though to strike.

I ducked, feeling my heart push up through my throat. Desperately trying to keep my wits about me, I flicked the flashlight back on. Praying to myself, not sure what I could even do with no weapon besides to scream for Joe, I turned the beam to my left, in the direction where the figure had stood.

I took in one breath, then another.

There was nothing there.

Relief flooded my body, but concern did, too. Okay, so the figure had moved—but where had it gone? I shone the light to the right, then to the left. I swiveled completely around and shone the light behind me. I turned in a circle, slowly, searching the whole area . . . as far as the flashlight's beam would reach.

Nothing.

My heart was still pounding in my chest, and my body, if not my head, was still convinced there was a threat nearby. I tried to recreate what I had seen in my mind's eye—a large human figure. Bulky. Arm raised. Dark clothing.

Was it possible he hadn't really been there?

Had I imagined the whole thing?

Just then, the sky opened up, and a torrent of rain began to pour down into the woods. I quickly aimed my flashlight at the tent and scurried back. I unzipped the tent but before I stepped inside, I slowly scanned the woods with my flashlight, checking one more time for the figure that had stood right beside me.

Nothing.

I chuckled to myself, trying to find it funny.

I'm getting as bad as Joe.

I ducked through the opening to the tent, zippering it tightly behind me.

"Frank!" Joe's voice pierced my dreams just a few hours later, after I'd finally drifted back to sleep once Joe began his second shift.

I blinked. "Wha—what, Joe? It can't be later than three."

Joe looked at his watch. "It's four, actually. Listen, Frank—do you hear that?"

I fell silent, perking up my ears. And then—yeah. I felt my whole body tense. Something was making lots of noise outside the tent—something was *trying* to make a lot of noise. Banging and stomping. Whoever was out there, he or she really wanted us to know they were there.

I sat straight up in my sleeping bag. "Do you think . . . ?"

Joe looked at me seriously. "*Someone's* out there, Frank," he insisted. "Someone wants us to *know* they're there. Did anything like this happen on your shift?"

I bit my lip, thinking, *Something even worse happened—I saw the guy.* But somehow I couldn't force the words from my mouth. Before I'd fallen asleep about an hour ago, I'd pretty much convinced myself I must have imagined the figure I saw. What would anyone be doing this deep in the woods? Why wouldn't I have seen him again?

"No," I whispered now. "But, Joe—we have to go out there."

Joe nodded grimly.

We both silently prepared, each holding a makeshift weapon—me with my flashlight, Joe with a huge branch he'd found while we'd searched for firewood and had insisted on keeping beside him in the tent. "You never know," he'd said ominously when I'd asked him why. Now I understood.

Careful not to make a sound, we approached the opening. The noise was still going on outside, loud as ever. Metallic clanking, like whoever was out there had found the pots and pans we'd hidden in a cooler with our food. We'd packed up everything, as instructed, so as not to leave anything to tempt the bears.

Joe glanced at me, then quickly unzipped the tent. Before I could say a word, he was out and on his feet. I quickly followed, shining a beam of light toward the cooler before I was even fully standing.

"Oh . . . gosh," Joe murmured, taking in the sight. "Well, now I feel stupid."

I stared in wonder at the creature by the cooler.

It was a raccoon. Tiny mask, striped tail, opposable thumbs—the whole works. The little troublemaker had the nerve to stare at us challengingly, as if opening up our cooler and playing with our pans was its God-given right.

"He ate all our apples," Joe said with dismay, standing on his tiptoes to look into the cooler. "Little bugger."

I moved forward then, advancing on the raccoon and yelling, "Scram! Get lost! Get out of our campsite, you little bandit!"

The raccoon looked slightly offended, but he cleared out.

For a moment I just stood there in the early morning darkness, breathing in the night air and feeling supremely silly. I'd gotten scared before—between the unfamiliar setting, the darkness, and the storm. The figure I'd seen—well, it was probably some kind of animal, too, right? Wasn't that the most logical explanation?

It had to be, I figured, as Joe and I secured our cooler and crawled back into our tent. I collapsed back onto my sleeping bag and tried to catch another hour or two of sleep before my shift came around. *Must have been an animal—it's the only logical explanation.*

Except.

What kind of animal is that big and travels on two feet?

"Your turn, Frank."

It seemed like I'd scarcely closed my eyes before my brother was waking me up for my second and final shift. It was six a.m. and the sun was out, albeit a little weak. Joe dropped gratefully back into his sleeping bag and was out before I'd left the tent. I unzipped the opening and squeezed out, thrilled to find the surroundings I remembered unharmed by the night and illuminated by beautiful, welcome sunshine.

I did a quick walk around our campgrounds—all intact except the apples that nasty raccoon had eaten. No sign of any kind of trespassing. I took a deep breath and smiled.

Don't think I've ever been so glad to see the sun.

I was hungry and could use something to eat. I kind of wanted coffee, too—something I didn't normally drink, but it was good for early mornings like this one. A coffeemaker wasn't included in our gear from ATAC, but I knew Joe had brought his trusty French press from home and wouldn't mind if I used it. I just needed to grab it from his backpack, then get a fire going and heat up some water.

I was about five feet away from the tent when I saw it, and my heart froze again. Right in front of the tent opening—scrawled messily in the mud, as though with a stick.

The letter *L*.

A chill ran over my whole body; I guess I was so scared I didn't hear the footsteps behind me.

Because just then, a deep, rough voice startled me out of my stupor:

"You shouldn'ta come."

Justin

I wasn't asleep for more than ten minutes before I woke up to the sound of raised voices outside our tent. I sighed and rubbed my eyes. Part of me was sad to see the morning, since I'd gotten, I figured, a grand total of three hours of sleep the night before. But a bigger part of me was glad to have that long night behind me. Granted, nothing had happened besides a visit from a hungry raccoon, but still . . . daylight was good. Daylight was *realllly* good.

It took me a minute to figure out that Frank was arguing with someone outside. Which was weird, to say the least, because we were in the middle of the wilderness and it couldn't be much later than six-thirty a.m. I quickly wiggled out of my sleeping bag and darted toward the tent opening. If Frank was out there arguing with a ghost . . . well, I could handle that if it were light outside.

". . . coupla city slickers just like all the rest of them," a tall, gaunt, elderly man was saying to Frank as I emerged from the tent. "They think, 'Oh! I like my backyard! I like . . . *birds*!'" He said "birds" with such scorn, you would think he was talking about synchronized swimming or something equally ridiculous. "'I think I'll go *camping*! That'll be a lark!'"

Frank was holding out his hands in front of him, like he might physically tamp down the man's anger. "Listen, sir, I promise you, we're not just tourists here. We're students. And we're here to—"

The man scowled. "To write a paper about those poor kids who died here. *I* know. I know just what you're up to."

I moved forward, attracting the man's attention for the first time. Hoping I might start this conversation over, I held out my hand. "Good morning, sir. I'm Joe Hardy. I see you've met my brother, Frank . . ."

The man turned to face me, still scowling. He had short, close-cropped silver hair and a neat, short silver beard. His expression, though—there was something *severe* about him. Maybe it was the intensity in his eyes or the slight hook to the end of his nose. Or maybe it was the fact that he looked like he wanted to cook and eat Frank and me for breakfast.

"I met Frank," the man said with a quick nod. After a brief hesitation, he held out his hand. "Farley O'Keefe. I'm the head ranger here at the park. Don't mean to be rude."

I nodded slowly, shaking his hand. "Nice to meet you, Farley."

He shook, then quickly stepped back. "It's just, those cases are sensitive things for me, you know. I've been here thirty years, and I remember every one of those kids who disappeared. No matter what you believe happened, there ain't nothing more tragic than a little child off and disappearing."

Frank glanced at me and nodded. "We absolutely agree, Farley. I hope you understand— we don't mean to disrespect any of the families that lost children. We just want to collect all the facts."

Farley scowled again and spit on the ground. "Sure, collect all the facts and tie them up with a nice little bow, so's you can come to some wild conclusion about what happened, right—some conspiracy theory? Or maybe a ghost story."

I glanced hesitantly at my brother. "We really don't *know* what happened yet, sir," I said slowly. "Maybe you can help us. What do you think happened?"

Farley turned to me then, his dark eyes seeming to bore into mine. "Don't patronize me, boy. I'll tell you what happened. It's what happens whenever city slickers who don't understand the wilderness come traipsing into my park. *They got hurt.* And you boys, you're no better'n any of them. By being here at all, by not knowing the woods, by not knowing your surroundings, you're putting yourselves at risk of ending up just like all of those kids."

I stumbled back, breaking his gaze. "Uh . . ."

"Are you saying we'll end up dead?" Frank asked. A note of alarm had crept into his normally calm voice.

Farley looked at him with suspicion for a moment, then he scowled. "Naw, I'm just sayin' you need to respect nature. Understand the risks. And to help you do that, I'd like to take you boys on a tour."

I glanced at my brother. A tour? With this crusty old park ranger? Would that help us or hurt us?

"I'll take you around to some of the campsites

where the kids disappeared," Farley went on. "Tell you what the risks were, what I think happened. How about that?"

Frank and I looked at each other again. I really didn't know what to say. Farley seemed to read our hesitation, and he sighed.

"Aw, c'mon," he said. "I'm not really all that bad, I promise. I've just been working in this park my whole career, and I don't like hearing people defame it with silly ghost stories, understand?"

Frank looked at Farley—he wore an open, almost hopeful expression—and then back at me.

"Okay," he said finally. "We'll go."

Farley drove an old dark green Jeep with MISTY FALLS STATE PARK stenciled on the driver side door. Frank climbed in the front and I climbed in the cramped backseat, and off we went. Farley, who seemed to be in a much better mood now that he was in charge, chattered on cheerfully about weather patterns, different types of trees, the birds we saw perched in their branches. When he started talking about animal life in the park, though, I perked up.

"We've got quite an assortment of wildlife here," Farley was saying, "and some not-altogether-friendly creatures among them. This park is home to three types of bears—black bears, grizzlies, and brown bears. We also have wolves, coyotes, bobcats, badgers, lynx, elks, moose, rattlesnakes, and wolverines." He paused, giving Frank a meaningful look. "But it's the bears you really have to worry about."

I piped up from the back. "Do you think all of the Misty Falls Lost were victims of bear attacks?"

Farley glanced at me in the rearview mirror, smiling slyly like he knew what I was getting at and he was having none of it. "I don't know exactly what happened to any of those poor children," he replied. "But I can lay out some scenarios." Pulling into a small lot, he parked the Jeep. "Come with me, boys. This is the first campsite."

One by one, we all piled out of the car and Frank and I followed Farley down a narrow path through the woods. We walked for some time, over rocks, even through a shallow stream, before reaching a small cleared area that, like our own site, hugged the rocky bank of the river.

Farley paused in the center and turned to face us. "Ten years ago," he announced, "the Bragg family camped here. It consisted of Mr. and Mrs. Bragg; their eight-year-old daughter, Kerry; and their five-year-old son, Danny. They were from Chicago, taking a camping tour of the American

West. This was only their second time ever camping. And they chose to camp in one of the most challenging parts of the park."

"What does that mean?" Frank asked. "Challenging?"

Farley shrugged. "It means there're all kinds of wildlife in this area. And the terrain is not easy. As you can see right there, there's a rocky drop-off leading down into the river. And how's the current look, boys?"

I looked. The water was moving rapidly, tiny whitecaps forming as it gushed around rocks and logs. "Pretty fast," I admitted.

"Right." Farley smiled. "Now, on that fateful night, two different grizzly bears were seen in this area. Did you know that?"

Frank and I shook our heads. "No."

Farley nodded. "And when campers arrive at the park, they're given instructions on how to deter bears—putting away all food in an airtight container, putting the food far from the tent. Do you know what the Braggs did?"

"No," I said, though this was starting to make me a little uncomfortable. The Braggs had lost a child—was Farley trying to imply that it was their own fault?

"They put their leftovers in a makeshift trash

container about ten feet from the tent," Farley said. "And they brought crackers and cookies into the tent for the kids to snack on. Any bear could have scented those from yards away."

I glanced at Frank. *Well.* I had to admit, Farley was definitely making it sound like Kerry's disappearance might have been a tragic accident or attack.

"Here's my theory," Farley went on. "In the middle of the night, little Kerry woke in her tent, which was placed here." He stood on the highest part of the campsite, about six feet from the rocky drop-off to the river. "She came out and went to use the latrine, which was over there." He pointed to a small copse of trees. "My belief, though, is that en route, Kerry encountered a hungry bear that was scoping their campground. Terrified, and not knowing how to react to bears, she ran as fast as she could in the opposite direction—forgetting the rocky riverbank, falling down, and getting picked up by the current." He paused, waiting for that to sink in.

I glanced at Frank. His expression seemed to confirm what I felt: Farley's scenario sounded pretty believable.

"Once she fell," Farley went on in a quieter voice, "that poor little girl was doomed. She may have hit her head and lost consciousness. She may have drowned in the current. Or maybe the bear went after her. Either way, she was gone."

I nodded slowly. "Well," I said finally, "your explanation makes a lot of sense." Farley nodded vigorously, and I went on, "I just wish we could know somehow what really happened."

Farley narrowed his eyes at me. "Come with me," he said. "I have more to show you."

We hurried back down the narrow path to the Jeep and hopped back in. Farley threw the vehicle into drive and we chugged out of the parking lot and down the main road of the park.

"Did you know," Farley said, "that in addition to the so-called Misty Falls Lost, six others have disappeared on the grounds over the last ten years, presumed victims of natural occurrences?"

"No," admitted Frank, "we didn't."

Farley nodded. "That's right. Of course they were all adults, so they didn't get the coverage the Misty Falls Lost did. They didn't fit the story the media wanted to tell. But this park is very, very dangerous, boys."

He stopped the Jeep again less than a mile from the first campsite.

"Detective Cole said all the abduction sites are along the river," I said, suddenly remembering his words. "Is that true?"

"It is," Farley agreed, climbing out of the Jeep. Frank and I followed. "I'm sure you know that bears frequent the rivers. Their own habitats aren't far from the river."

"And," Frank went on, adding to my recollection, "Detective Cole said in each case, a bear had been spotted in the area within two days."

Farley nodded. "That's right," he agreed. "Now what does that make you think?"

I caught Frank's eye. *No idea, but I know what you want it to make me think.*

With Frank and me hot on his heels, Farley led us down an even narrower, more overgrown path through some low brush, bushes, and weeds. "Sorry about all this," he said, taking out a huge white-handled knife from his belt and slicing off a branch that jutted into the path, scratching all of our ankles. "This site hasn't gotten much use in the last couple years. I'm sure you can imagine why."

"The park must be losing a lot of camping business because of this story," Frank suggested.

"That's right. And that's less revenue for the park, and less we get to spend protecting the grounds and everything that lives on it."

With Farley using his knife to thin out the scrub, it was easier going, and within twenty minutes we arrived at a small, clear area with a low, flat rock that led right into the river. Farley turned to face us.

"Seven years ago, five-year-old Sarah Finnegan disappeared from this site. Earlier that day, a hiker had reported seeing a grizzly female and her cub not fifty yards from here. That night, against ranger advice, Sarah and her older sister, Justine, slept out in the open, 'under the stars' as her parents called it. At around three a.m., Justine reported being awoken by a loud noise. Sarah was gone. By the time Justine woke her parents and they searched the area, there was no sign of Sarah—just her pillow floating in the river."

I cleared my throat. "And what do you think happened to her?"

Farley turned to me, his expression grave. "I don't think the noise her sister heard was man-made, let me put it that way," he replied.

I sighed. I had to admit, Farley was convincing me—there *were* always bears in the area. That had to be significant. And while I knew the families that had lost children never would have intentionally done anything to put their child in danger, it sounded like they had made some silly decisions.

Farley spoke again, his voice lower now: "Camping out here in nature without understanding the risks is a lot like diving into the ocean without knowing how to swim," he said. "The ocean doesn't *want* to hurt you. But you gotta respect its power. I believe those poor families that came here, came here expecting some Disney World vacation. But nature isn't like that. You gotta know how to protect yourself."

I glanced at Frank, who looked skeptical. "Of course," he said, "that doesn't account for Justin's reappearance. If he had been attacked by a bear—or fallen victim to a tragic accident—he couldn't have shown up completely healthy, completely *alive* four days ago, now could he?"

Farley shrugged, frowning at the ground. "I can't say I know what happened to that poor boy. I can only say that whatever happened, it doesn't make me believe any less that *most* of these disappearances were natural. Maybe that boy survived a bear attack somehow, and he was living in the woods . . ."

"Living in the woods on his own for twelve years, so close to civilization?" I prodded. "And with nice manners and good language skills? That's an interesting theory, Farley, but I don't think it holds up."

Farley looked up at me and shrugged. Surprisingly, there was no anger in his expression. "I suppose you're right," he agreed. "But all that means to me is there's a lot to be learned about that boy. Last I heard, even his daddy wasn't totally sure— they were doing some tests to find out if he's really Justin. Anyhow, I don't think it means anything bigger about all the disappearances."

Frank nodded. "Fair enough. But there's something else your theory doesn't explain, either— what about the word 'lost' that was scrawled in the dirt at the campsites where children went missing?"

Farley rolled his eyes. "Come on, now. You boys are fallin' for that Hollywood nonsense?"

"Nonsense?" I asked. "But I thought . . ."

Farley scowled again. "Do your research, boys. The 'lost' myth is just that, a myth. It's something the media made up to beef up the story, and all the eyewitnesses who reported it just *happened* to report it after seeing it on the news. I don't think anyone involved with the case seriously thinks it really happened."

I caught Frank's eye. *Innnnteresting.*

Suddenly, there was a loud beeping sound. I jumped, startled, before realizing the loud noise was coming from . . . my pants! Suddenly understanding what it was, I whipped my phone out of my pocket.

"You have gotta be kiddin' me," Farley grumbled. "You even get reception out here?"

"Some," I said vaguely, clicking open my phone. I didn't want to tell Farley that the souped-up cell phones ATAC supplied us with work everywhere. "Hello?"

"Joe, it's Rich. I know it's early, but—"

"It's fine," I replied, looking back at Farley, who was now eagerly showing Frank something about the river and the way the campsite was situated on it. "As it happens, we were already up."

"Rough night, huh?" Rich replied, but he continued before I could respond. "Listen, I need you boys to come to the hospital as soon as possible. There's been an important development."

"What's that?" I asked, hoping that somehow Rich had learned something that would solve the whole nature vs. man debate. After spending the morning with Farley, I was less sure than ever of what had happened to these kids.

"The DNA results are in," he told me. "Justin is definitely the same boy who disappeared twelve years ago. And the doctors are hoping the results might press him to remember something."

Something Wild

F arley wouldn't hear of us taking a cab to the hospital or waiting for Rich to come pick us up. When he heard that we were needed at the hospital, he insisted on driving us into town himself.

"Shoot," he said, putting the Jeep into gear as we bumped over the main road of the park toward the exit. "I don't suppose it'll take me twenty minutes, there and back. And I want to make sure you boys get the *real* facts for this paper of yours."

Actually, once we were off the subject of the Misty Falls Lost, Farley wasn't so bad. He told us about his long career as a ranger and his long marriage to his wife, Sylvie, who had died just eighteen months ago. They had a son, Sean—but he had died years ago, serving in the army during Desert Storm.

"It's a heck of a thing," Farley said, his voice strained, "to lose a child. I know how hard it was for Sylvie and me, and I know how tough it must be for all these poor parents of the children who were lost in my park." He paused and looked at me, his eyes sincere. "I just don't think it helps no one to make up stories and legends and call this anything besides what it was—a tragic accident."

"*Several* tragic accidents," Joe put in from the backseat.

Farley blinked, then nodded. "Several. That's right. I've seen a lot of terrible things happen in my park, boys. Those children—those just might be the worst. But I've seen enough to know that bears *do* attack, people *do* slip and fall and die, people *do* drown. Nature is beautiful and I love that park with all my heart. But she's dangerous, too. She's dangerous. You remember that, boys, all right?"

He'd pulled into the parking lot and now edged the Jeep into a parking space.

"Are you coming in?" I asked as Farley put the Jeep in park and shut down the ignition.

Farley looked a little caught off guard by my

question, but he nodded curtly. "One of my good friends," he said, "just had gallbladder surgery. I s'pose I'll go in and see how the nurses are treatin' him. Why do you look so surprised, boy?"

I blinked and shrugged. I hadn't realized I did look surprised—though maybe I was a little surprised that Farley, who seemed so skeptical of anything to do with the "so-called" Misty Falls Lost, was coming into the hospital that housed Justin. And there was something else, too. There was something . . . *wild* about Farley. I could see him tracking a bear, I could see him making fire with two sticks, I could see him gutting a rabbit and cooking it for dinner (whether he even liked rabbit, of course, I didn't know)—but I couldn't really see him entering a hospital with a cheery face and a "get well soon" balloon. Of course that was my own weird bias, though. It only made sense that Farley was connected to this town; he'd lived here for decades.

Farley grinned mischievously as we walked to the entrance. "You surprised I have friends, are ya?"

I shook my head. "No, sir. I find you delightful."

Farley laughed then, a deep, long laugh that he had to throw back his head to let out. When he finished, he clapped me on my shoulder. "I suppose you're all right," he told me, "for a city slicker."

Joe caught my eye and smiled—he knew me well enough to know that I hadn't been trying to make a joke. I just liked Farley. Still, I seemed to have gained points with the old man.

Farley accompanied us to the psych floor, explaining that his friend's room was just one floor above: "I s'pose I can escort you boys to the right nurses' station, make sure they don't mistake you for more lost children." When we reached the nurses' station and explained that we were looking for Detective Cole, the ponytailed nurse at the front desk held up her hand. "Just a moment. We'll let him know and someone will be right with you."

We waited for a few minutes before a familiar curly-haired candy striper passed by the station. "Well hello there," said Chloe, looking from Joe (briefly) to me. Her eyes stayed on me for a moment, or maybe I was just imagining things.

"Hello, Chloe," I said, hoping I didn't have a goofy grin on my face.

"Are you here to see Justin?" she asked. "You heard the news, right? That it's definitely him?"

I nodded. "It's really exciting," I said, which right after I said it I realized sounded ridiculous. *Really exciting?* Like this was a roller coaster I couldn't wait to ride? "I mean . . . I'm glad his parents are sure now. I mean . . ."

Chloe nodded. "It *is* exciting for what this means about memory," she said. "I've been talking to Dr. Carrini about it. If he really *is* Justin, then it means he really *has* repressed so many of his memories. We're trying hard to get them back. In fact, Dr. Carrini wants to have an interview with Justin in a few minutes—just to talk to him, to see if the test results trigger anything."

Behind me, Farley huffed. I'd actually forgotten he was back there. "They haven't *told* the boy yet?" he asked, clearly disapproving.

Chloe glanced at him. "Er . . . no, not yet. Dr. Carrini wanted everyone here. Oh . . ." She looked behind us, relief crossing her face. "Here he is. I'm sure he'll fill you in. Frank, Joe, I'm sure I'll see you in there." She smiled warmly, looking right into my eyes, and then walked off.

In the few seconds before Dr. Carrini reached us, Joe let out a low whistle.

Farley snorted. "No kidding," he muttered, squinting at me. "Boy, you're red enough to blend in with a fire engine."

Before I could defend myself, Dr. Carrini breezed between us and smiled at Frank and me. If he even noticed Farley was there, he made no indication.

"Boys," he said, "I'm glad you could make it.

Detective Cole is back in the room with Justin and his parents. We're just about to tell him the results of the DNA testing, which confirm that he is, in fact, Justin Greer."

I nodded.

"Interesting," said Joe.

Dr. Carrini went on: "It's my hope that this will trigger some memories in Justin. Now that he knows we're not lying to him or making assumptions—there's no denying that he is these folks' child. Because I have to be honest with you, boys—I'm beginning to worry about Justin's memory."

Farley spoke up: "You mean you're afraid the boy won't ever remember who he is?" he asked. He looked saddened by that news, and I filed that little piece of info away. It seemed Farley really *was* sympathetic to the missing kids and their parents. That made him less of a suspect in my book.

Dr. Carrini frowned at him. "I'm sorry. You are?"

Farley held out his hand. "Farley O'Keefe, park ranger for thirty years," he said, forcefully grabbing the doctor's hand and shaking it hard. "I been showin' these boys around."

Dr. Carrini tipped his head. "I see. Well, yes,

Mr. O'Keefe, I am beginning to wonder whether Justin will ever truly remember who he is. Even if he recovers some memories, at this point, I fear he may always have gaps."

Joe furrowed his brow. "And the cause of that would be . . .?"

The doctor shrugged. "Well, that's what we hope to learn, boys. There are many potential causes. Head injury. Drug abuse. But in the meantime, let's stay positive: I hope we *will* be able to help Justin remember today."

I heard running footsteps and looked up to see Rich coming up behind Dr. Carrini. "Oh, good," he said, looking at Joe and me with relief. "You two made it. And hey there, Farley."

Farley nodded.

Rich touched the doctor's shoulder and lowered his voice. "Listen, Edie and Jacob are very eager to start this. Things are getting a little tense in there. Can we begin?"

Dr. Carrini agreed quickly. "Sure. Come on, boys. Let's get this started."

We moved to follow them down the hall, but Rich paused and gestured to Farley. "You want to come, Farley? I know you must be curious about the boy. You certainly went through enough with these investigations."

I expected Farley to scowl and refuse, but when I turned, the expression on his face was hard to describe. It was a mixture of a lot of things—loss, anger, vulnerability, but most of all, sadness. "No, Richard," he said softly, shaking his head and clearing his throat. "I'm on my way out. See you, boys."

He spun around and had gotten halfway down the hall before we could reply.

"Wow," Joe murmured, giving me a sideways glance. "I guess he really *does* have a heart."

I nodded, turning to Rich. "Mr. O'Keefe is a . . . an interesting guy."

Rich snorted. "Yeah, he sure is. One heck of a town character, he is. But a decent guy." He paused. "He lost a son years ago, you know."

"He told us," Joe said with a nod. "Killed in the first Iraq war."

Rich nodded. "I always thought . . . well. Of course no one wants to see children hurt. But I think all these disappearances . . . they took a special toll on Farley. Because of what he'd been through with his son."

I nodded. For a moment, we were all quiet.

"Anyway," Rich went on as we stood in front of Justin's door. "Let's see if we can't solve some mysteries."

• • •

Inside Justin's room, Edie sat at his bedside, stroking his hand and flipping through a family album. Justin was looking at the pictures politely, but with no emotion in his eyes. Beside his bed, I noticed, was a small piece of wood that slightly resembled an elk, with a whittling knife beside it. Rich followed my gaze and nodded.

"Another secret talent of Justin's," he whispered to me. "We discovered it last night."

Hmmm. Where might Justin have learned to whittle? Or had he taught himself? It was an interesting clue, but—like everything we had learned about Justin so far—it didn't seem to lead us in any specific direction.

On the other side of the room, by the window, Jacob sat with his nose in a *Gearhead* magazine. Every so often he would peek over the top, but he always seemed disappointed by what he saw Justin doing. I stepped into the room and was surprised to find *another* man—around the same age as Jacob and Edie but with short, grayish hair and a neat mustache—standing against the wall next to the door. He glanced up at me glancing at him.

"Hank Stapleton," he introduced himself, holding out his hand. "I'm Edie's husband. And you two . . . ?"

Rich stepped in. "These are the boys come to write a paper about the missing children, Hank," he said gently. "Edie and Jacob said they didn't mind if I brought 'em in."

Hank looked surprised, but he nodded absently. "Okay then," he said, forcing a smile. "Nice to meet you boys."

"Likewise," said Joe with an apologetic smile.

"All right," announced Dr. Carrini, pulling up a chair to sit beside Justin, opposite Edie. "Justin, I've gathered your friends and family here because we have something to announce to you," he said.

Justin frowned, turning to Edie, but Dr. Carrini reached over and took his face in his hands and guided Justin's eyes back to him. "Listen, Justin," he went on. "It's very important that you focus on me when I'm talking to you. Understand?"

Justin stared at him, his expression a bit confused but still mostly blank. "Okay."

"What?"

"I understand."

Dr. Carrini nodded. "Good. Your social skills are getting better. Now, Justin, do you remember the tests we ran a couple days ago? I took a swab of cells from inside your mouth."

"I remember," Justin agreed. He turned his head just slightly, seeking out Jacob, who'd put down the magazine and was watching with a pained expression. "*That* man doesn't think I'm his son."

Jacob coughed. "It's not that. I just want to be su—"

Dr. Carrini turned to hush Jacob. "Mr. Greer. Please let me direct the session."

Jacob looked stung. "Okay," he muttered, and he grabbed his magazine again, holding it in his lap.

Dr. Carrini turned back to Justin, who now was looking directly at the doctor again. "Now, Justin, we have the results of those tests. Those tests have proven, my boy, that you are *Justin Greer*. There can be no doubt now." He paused. Justin opened his mouth and closed it. He looked down at the sheets and began fiddling with the top one. He looked confused, as though he understood he was supposed to have some kind of reaction but felt none.

I caught Joe's eye across the room. He looked as uncomfortable as I felt.

"These are your *parents*, Justin," Dr. Carrini went on, gesturing to Edie and Jacob. "Jacob, please come closer. Look at them, Justin." He paused. Jacob put down his magazine again and shuffled toward the bed. He and Edie both looked at their son, their expressions nakcd and sad, hoping for even the tiniest sign of recognition.

"Justin," Dr. Carrini went on, "I want you to think hard. Do you remember these people? Do you remember anything about them?"

Justin stared hard at Edie, then at Jacob, his eyes wide. He looked pained, like he was literally searching every crevice of his mind. But I could see from his expression that he wasn't finding what he knew he should.

"No," he said finally. And he pulled away, looking back at his sheets.

I let out a deep breath. For a moment, it felt like all the air had been let out of the room. Nobody said a word, but you could feel the change in the atmosphere. After a moment, Edie started to weep.

I looked to Jacob, who seemed completely stunned. His face was still arranged in the same hopeful expression from just moments before, but his eyes had turned dark.

"No!" he cried finally, slapping his hand down on the edge of the bed. Edie sobbed louder.

Dr. Carrini was backing up his chair, and he held out his hands. "Now, Jacob," he said, his voice low and bland. "You know—"

"I don't know nothin'!" Jacob shouted, his furious eyes turning on Dr. Carrini. "I don't know why this boy survived, only to turn into someone

I don't know! And I don't know how to be a father to this—to this *wild thing* when he doesn't even remember who I am!"

Edie sobbed even louder. Hank moved away from his spot on the wall, taking her in his arms.

"I don't know what I'm supposed to do now," Jacob went on, his eyes boring into Dr. Carrini's, his voice ragged with emotion, "with a wife who's forgotten who I am and a boy who'll never remember me. Who'll never be *normal*."

Edie cried out then, and she suddenly pushed Hank away from her. "Let me go, let me go," she begged. "I can't take this another second."

She jumped up from her spot in the chair, then darted from the room. Hank hesitated for just a moment before following her. Jacob was sniffling, and he wiped furiously at his eyes.

Justin picked silently at the sheets. If the proceedings had bothered him at all, if he had even *noticed* them, he made no sign of it. A few seconds after Edie left, he picked up the wood figure and the knife from the table by his bed and started whittling.

It was then that I felt Joe's hand on my shoulder. "Let's go," he urged.

Of course he was right. We probably should have excused ourselves minutes before. This was all too personal for us to witness. But I had been too stunned by what had happened to react.

Nodding at Rich and Dr. Carrini, we left the room.

"Wow," Joe whispered when we were out of earshot. "I know we've witnessed a lot of sad things before, but . . . *wow*."

"I know," I agreed. "I know we were hoping to hear something that would help our investigation, but I almost wish we could go back in time and stay at the park. That felt . . . *raw*."

"Those poor people," agreed Joe.

We continued strolling down the hallway, back to the nurses' station. Right before we got there, Hank spotted us as he was walking back toward the room.

"Boys," he said with a nod as we drew closer. "I'm . . . I'm sorry you had to witness that."

"Don't be," Joe said. "We're sorry this must be so difficult for you and your wife. You have our sympathy."

Hank sighed. He was a gentle-looking man, especially compared with Jacob's gruffness. His hair and mustache were neat and well-trimmed, he wore a yellow polo shirt and khakis, and even his fingernails were impeccable. If Jacob looked like a bit of a mountain man, Hank looked like a soccer dad from the suburbs.

"Do you live near here?" I asked.

He shrugged. "Somewhat," he said with a weary smile. "We live about two hours away in Boise. These last few days have been tough—we didn't want to uproot our kids. So Edie's been here, and I've been taking care of them and traveling back and forth. Thank goodness for my sister's family taking the kids sometimes, or I wouldn't be able to come up at all."

Joe nodded. "I don't mean to pry, but do your kids know what's going on? Have you told them about Justin?"

Hank shook his head. "No, that's a fair question. We haven't. Didn't want to get them all excited about a brother if . . . well." He looked at the floor and sighed deeply. "It's been a tough week."

"It must be tough to see your wife in pain," I suggested.

"*Very* tough." Hank agreed. "And there's nothing I can do. I can only imagine how I would feel to lose one of our children, then get him back years later, but he doesn't remember me." He frowned and added quietly, "And you see what Jacob is like."

Joe and I glanced at each other, unsure how to respond. "He seems . . . challenging," I said finally.

"He's not exactly Mr. Sensitivity, let's put it that way," Hank scoffed, shaking his head. "And he's always been like that. Way Edie tells it, that had a lot to do with their split." He paused, looking from me to Joe. "You boys need a ride back to camp? Edie's down in the chapel—says she needs to be alone. Maybe once I take you boys out and come back, everyone will be in a better mood."

I nodded. "If you're willing, that would be great."

"No problem," Hank said, pulling a set of car keys out of his pocket. "I'm right this way."

We followed him down the corridor toward the exit. Joe looked like he was hesitating—like he wanted to say something, but he kept biting his lip. I looked at him like, *What?* Finally he spoke: "Maybe," he said, "I mean, I don't want to presume, but maybe Jacob will get better over the next few days, you know?" he asked, looking thoughtful.

"What do you mean?" asked Hank. He didn't look offended—just curious.

"I mean, now Jacob has hard evidence that this is his own flesh and blood," Joe went on. "Maybe it's not just a matter of Justin recognizing Jacob—maybe Jacob needs to recognize his son a bit, too."

We had walked out into the parking lot, and

Hank gazed up into the afternoon sun, looking thoughtful. "Maybe you're right," he said. "Although, there's one major problem with that theory. No matter what, Justin isn't Jacob's flesh and blood."

I frowned. "What?" I asked. "I thought they tested his DNA against Jacob's and Edie's."

"No." Hank shook his head. "They tested his DNA against *Justin's*—against a lock of hair Edie kept in his baby book." He paused, looking at us curiously. "They really never told you?" he asked, shaking his head.

"Told us what?" Joe asked.

"Justin isn't Edie and Frank's biological son," Hank explained. "He's adopted."

JOE

7

Someone Was Here

As soon as we got back to our campsite, it was time for Frank and me to play a little game of What Did We Learn Today And Who Are Our Suspects?

"Well," I began as soon as we were well out of earshot of anyone in the parking lot and headed down the trail back to camp, "that Farley sure is a ray of sunshine."

Frank smiled. "He's a crusty one, that's for sure. But you know, he seems to have a soft side, too."

I nodded. "When he was talking about his son, I felt so terrible for him. You could see how much it hurt him."

"Yeah," Frank agreed, "and back at the hospital,

100

when they were talking about Justin—I dunno. It seems to me that Farley was really hurt by these children's disappearances, deep down. He seemed almost like . . . he couldn't *handle* knowing more about Justin."

I hadn't seen it that way, but now that Frank said it, I remembered the look in Farley's eyes as he'd abruptly left the hospital. "I guess so," I said, then paused before adding, "though he's still a suspect, in my mind."

SUSPECT PROFILE

Name: Farley O'Keefe

Hometown: Misty Falls, Idaho

Physical Description: 6'0", short gray hair, close-cropped beard, grizzled expression

Occupation: Park ranger

Background: Lost a son in Desert Storm; lost a wife eighteen months ago. Says he understands the pain of parents who lost children

Suspicious behavior: An almost pathological dedication to convincing visitors the Misty Falls Lost were victims of natural accidents

"What do you mean?" asked Frank. "You think Farley might have done something to the kids who disappeared?"

I shook my head, although now that he said it, I wasn't totally sure *what* Farley might have done. "I just . . . think he knows something. I can't quite put my finger on it. I can't imagine him hurting a kid, but then, we don't know that much about him."

"And it's in Farley's best interest to deny any crimes were committed," Frank pointed out. "You could argue that's not really suspicious behavior, coming from him."

I nodded. "I guess. I just want to keep my eye on him. He's quite a character."

Frank rolled his eyes. "Speaking of characters," he said, "let's discuss Jacob."

I sighed. "He's . . . troubling."

SUSPECT PROFILE

Name: Jacob Greer

Hometown: Doddsville, Idaho

Physical description: 5'10", shaggy salt-and-pepper hair, brown eyes. A little heavy, rough around the edges

Occupation: Sporting equipment salesman

Background: Justin's adoptive father; ex-husband of Edie; lives alone

Suspicious behavior: Refused to believe Justin is really his son; when DNA tests proved it, had a tantrum and claimed Justin will never be "normal"

Suspected of: Having a reason to fear Justin's reappearance. Maybe Justin knows something he'd rather not go public

Possible motive: Self-protection

"Agreed," said Frank. "I know we can't imagine what he's going through right now. To lose a child, then gain him back, only to lose him again when he has no memory of you . . . that has to be very, very difficult."

"They don't make a greeting card for that one," I added.

"Definitely not. But his behavior is . . ."

"Angry," I suggested.

"Cold," added Frank.

"Almost like he's trying to sabotage something," I added. "He almost seems . . . *afraid* of Justin. Like he doesn't want to believe Justin is his son and he'll remember him."

Frank nodded, looking thoughtful. "Maybe that's totally normal," he suggested. "Maybe he's afraid."

"Or maybe," I suggested, "he has something to hide. Maybe he has a reason *not* to want Justin to come back."

Frank sighed, like it pained him to go down this path. "You really think he might have something to do with his own son's abduction, though?"

"I don't know," I admitted. "That seems far-fetched. And even if he did, that doesn't tell us anything about the other seven kids who went missing. But I think . . . like Farley, maybe he knows more than he's letting on."

Frank looked unhappy. "Never assume anyone is telling the truth," he said, reciting from the ATAC handbook.

"They have no reason to be straight with us . . . not if it could hurt them down the line," I added.

With that depressing thought, we returned to our camp. After the primer on bear attacks we'd gotten from Farley earlier that day, we were both inspired to safety-up our campsite, disposing of any food remnants and storing anything that looked potentially interesting to a bear in an aluminum cooler that ATAC had provided us.

"Does this look interesting to a bear?" I asked Frank, holding up a pack of gum I'd fished out of my backpack.

"Are you kidding?" asked Frank, elbow-deep in his own backpack. "Do I look like I know what a bear thinks? If you're wondering at all, put it in the cooler."

After totally ridding our tent of bear-attracting items and taking quick naps to make up for the sleep we lost last night, we were soon cooking our dinner over a roaring fire as the sun set.

I looked around at the darkening woods, my heart quickening. "I know it's silly," I said, "but I'm getting nervous the darker it's getting. I don't know why nighttime is so much scarier out here than at home. It's not like anything happened last night."

Frank was quiet for a minute. He pushed his foil-wrapped potato closer to the fire and seemed to think for a minute before replying, "Right."

"I guess you have the first shift tonight," I added, taking a sip of water.

"No problem," Frank agreed.

It wasn't long before I was climbing into my sleeping bag and Frank was settling down with a flashlight and his magazine. "Goodnight, bro," I said, my eyelids already growing heavy. "See you in three hours."

After all my nervousness, the first part of the night was kind of an anticlimax. The woods were totally silent, except for the occasional wind, and even when I peered outside the tent, having trouble believing that *nothing* weird was happening, a silent, motionless campsite greeted me.

"Your turn, bro," I told Frank when I woke him for his second shift.

Frank blinked, then wiped his eyes, sitting up. "Did anything . . . happen?" he asked.

"Nope," I said with a mock sigh. "I guess you were right about ghosts not being real and all."

He smirked at me, and I climbed back into my sleeping bag for a welcome second shift of sleep.

• • •

Frank woke me at four a.m. for my final shift of watching the campsite. It was still pitch dark, and I marveled at how long the night seemed when you were actually awake for half of it. "How was . . . ," I began asking Frank once I'd wiggled out of my sleeping bag, but he was already curled up in his own bag, fast asleep.

I knew we were supposed to be roughing it out in the wilderness, but when I was going to be up half the night, I needed video games. Muting the sound, I pulled out my handheld gaming device and got lost in the latest racing game. After a while, Frank's snoring and the occasional wind whipping through the trees lulled me into, if not total calm, then at least a pretty relaxed state.

Then I heard it. The sound was so jarring in the near-silent woods, I dropped my video game.

A car door slamming.

We were a good ten- or fifteen-minute walk from the parking lot, but I knew the roads that ran through the park were pretty extensive, and it was probably possible to drive closer to our site. The slam wasn't right nearby—it was like hearing one of your distant neighbors heading off on a quiet morning. But in such a serene area, the sound was unmistakable.

Don't freak, I told myself as my heart sped up. *Maybe it's Farley chasing after a bear. Maybe it's somebody heading to one of the other campsites.*

Then I heard the footsteps.

They were slow, deliberate. Coming out of the woods and heading for our tent. Heavy, like the person was large and not interested in disguising his or her approach.

I felt my heart jump into my throat.

I grabbed my flashlight and turned it on.

The footsteps stopped.

My heart pounding, I tried to sit perfectly still for a few minutes, just listening. I knew whoever made those footsteps was probably out there, staring at my silhouette against the illuminated tent. It seemed like hours but was probably only a couple minutes . . . no footsteps. No sounds at all, except the wind in the trees. Had I imagined the whole thing?

I thought about waking Frank, but then I remembered the night before: the raccoon incident. Not my proudest moment. No, before I woke Frank, I should at least peek outside the tent and see if there was anything suspicious out there. Grabbing the flashlight, I stood and waited for a moment to see if the footsteps would start up again. They didn't. So in one quick motion, before

I could second-guess myself, I zipped open the tent and stepped outside.

I noticed it right away. Our fire pit! When we'd gone to sleep, it had been burned out but neat—charred logs in the middle, fresh firewood and kindling piled off to the side. But now, it looked like someone had charged right through the middle—kicking the logs and kindling while they went! Worse, there were footprints, very big and very human, in the dirt and leading off into the woods.

Someone had been here. *Someone* who wanted us to know.

I felt my heart start to pound again. And just then, I heard them. Footsteps! Someone was running through the woods, just yards away! Springing into action, I ran after the mystery man, still clutching my flashlight. If someone was trying to mess with us—whether to hurt us or just frighten us—I wanted to find out who!

My feet pounded against the uneven ground as I struggled to keep up with the intruder and not trip on the rocks and undergrowth. In the distance, I could see the stranger who'd disturbed our campsite: a large man dressed all in black. I couldn't see his face, though—he was too far ahead and wearing a knit cap. Whoever he was, the intruder was making a beeline through the forest—we weren't on any sort of a path. He splashed through a shallow creek, and I followed. He vaulted over a fallen tree, and I was just seconds behind him.

Finally I heard feet slapping on pavement, and I knew he'd reached the road. Sure enough, seconds later I was standing at the edge of the park's main road, looking left and right. Where was he? Just then, a few feet down the road, I heard an engine pealing out as a huge black SUV roared into motion. It sped down the road toward, I assumed, the exit—and away from me.

I stood there for a few seconds after the SUV was out of sight, trying to calm myself.

Someone was really there. Someone was invading our campsite.

As frightened as I'd been of whatever befell the Misty Falls Lost, I still couldn't believe it.

After catching my breath, I turned around and tried to pick my way back to the campsite. It was slow going, trying to retrace my steps with no perspective and no trail to follow. All in all, it was probably a good half hour before I found our tent again. The first light of morning was just starting to break through the trees.

I sighed, walking up to the tent. I'd never been so relieved to see the sun!

But then, as I walked toward the tent, I stopped dead.

There. On the ground. Right before the tent entrance.

Am I seeing things?

No. And the sight brought fresh horror to my thumping heart.

Someone had scrawled letters in the damp dirt: *LO*

Two Nights, Two Letters

I woke to the sound of my brother screaming. Within seconds he was inside the tent. "Frank, wake up. Frank . . ."

"What's going on?" I asked, sitting up in my sleeping bag and rubbing my eyes. I'd only gone back to sleep about an hour before.

Joe looked like he'd seen a ghost. He looked at me, pale-faced and breathing hard. "Someone was here, Frank."

"Here where?" I asked, then gestured outside the tent. "*Here* here?"

"Yeah." Joe paused for a minute, trying to catch his breath. "And they left something." He stood up and headed for the exit and without a word, I followed.

He stopped just a few feet from the tent and turned around. "Look!"

I took just one step away, then turned around. He was gesturing to the ground right before the tent entrance. "Oh, man," I whispered.

This time it was clear as day. Someone had scrawled *LO* in the dirt with a stick. There was no mistaking the letters.

"It gets worse," Joe went on, giving me a grave look. "I heard a car about half an hour ago, then footsteps approaching the tent. It was still dark, so I turned on my flashlight. The footsteps stopped right away. But when I came out to look I saw that someone had run right through our fire pit. And then I heard them start up again—footsteps running through the woods. I followed them, and I saw the guy—big, wearing all black with a ski mask. I trailed him about half a mile to the road, then he got into a big black SUV and drove away."

I just stood there for a moment, taking all this in. Joe had seen an intruder, too. That meant there was no denying it anymore.

"Someone's trying to scare us," I said aloud.

Joe looked at me, then nodded slowly. "You think?" he asked.

"Isn't it obvious?" I asked. "The *L-O* must be a reference to the *L-O-S-T* that was supposedly scrawled outside the tents of the kids who disappeared."

"But Farley said that didn't really happen to all of them," Joe pointed out.

"It doesn't matter," I said. "Whoever's doing this knows we know about it. And they're trying to scare us—to make us think we're under attack, too."

Joe took a slow breath. "You think they're just trying to scare us," he said, "as opposed to really wanting to hurt us? I mean, who knows what that guy had in mind? Maybe I interrupted him before he could do us in and write the full 'lost' outside our tent."

I shook my head. "Come on, Joe," I said, "we're teenagers, not little kids. Besides, I think I saw an *L* scrawled outside the tent yesterday morning. Whoever's doing this is leaving one letter at a time."

Joe looked at me, shocked. "You saw an *L* yesterday and didn't tell me?" he asked.

I shrugged, feeling a little guilty. "I thought maybe it was left by the rain," I admitted, "or that it was a piece of an animal track. You know, on its own, *L* doesn't look like much."

Joe stared at the *LO*, then nodded. "Two nights, two letters," he said. "That means we have two more days to figure this whole thing out." He paused, then looked at me. "Then we become 'lost,'" he went on, "and who knows what will happen then?"

About two hours later, Joe and I were sitting in Rich's office in the Misty Falls Police Station. He'd listened to our tale from the night before and now frowned in thought.

"Interesting," he said, scratching his cheek. "Well, it does sound like someone's trying to mess with you boys. Because Farley told you the truth—we only saw the word 'lost' on one victim's campsite, and we think the others may have been fabrications."

"Lies," Joe translated.

Rich sighed. "Not lies, exactly. When you have a case like this, everyone wants to be the one to help solve it. And after the media started reporting that one 'lost' case, suddenly people started remembering it in others. Even though none of our officers at the scene saw it, and these people didn't 'remember' it until months or years later." He paused. "Whoever's leaving it for you boys, though, knows that *you* heard about it, and that's all that matters. If you know the legend of Nathan and the Misty Falls Lost, it'll scare you. And that's what he wants."

"Rich," I said, "can you tell us more about the other kids who disappeared? We've been focusing so heavily on Justin, I wonder if there's something we're missing."

He nodded. "Sure," he said. "Here's the rundown . . .

"Kerry, an eight-year-old girl, went missing the year after Justin. Her younger brother reported that she left the tent to use the restroom and never came back. Police found bare footprints leaving the tent but never found her remains. (Hers is also the case where "lost" was photographed scrawled on the ground outside the tent.)

"Sarah, a five-year-old girl, disappeared two years later. She slept outside with her older sister. Her sister reported being awoken by a loud noise in the middle of the night. Her sister's sleeping bag was empty, her pillow had been thrown in the creek, and there was no further evidence. (Sarah is the girl whose "remains" were found downriver several years later.)

"Luke, a seven-year-old boy, was frightened by a middle-of-the-night thunderstorm the following year and went to sleep in the car with his parents. Both parents remembered him joining them in the car, but in the morning, his bedding was gone and so was he—no further evidence was ever found.

"Alice, a four-year-old girl, is the only child to have disappeared during the day. She went for a walk with her teenage brother. Hours later, the brother was found unconscious from a blow to the head, lying in the middle of a trail only a quarter mile from the campsite. Alice was missing and no further evidence was found.

"Tommy, an eight-year-old boy, was dared by his younger brother to go outside the tent to investigate a noise (believed by police to have been an animal of some kind, based on the kid's description). He never returned, and there was no evidence.

"Kyle, a five-year-old boy, was simply missing from the tent in the morning. His teddy bear was missing, but his sleeping bag was intact. No evidence was found.

"Ellie, a six-year-old girl, is the most recent to have disappeared, only last year. Hers is the most startling case: It appears that someone or something cut a hole in the tent where she was sleeping and removed her. A fragment of her nightgown was found a few feet from the tent."

When Rich finished, I took a deep breath. "Well," I said. "These cases are pretty tragic."

"And creepy," Joe added. "Even if these were bear attacks, it seems weird that so little evidence was found."

Rich nodded. "That's probably where the ghost rumor comes from," he admitted. "What else could leave so little evidence behind? But no, it is possible for bears to leave very little. And bears were spotted near all of these campsites within forty-eight hours of the disappearances."

I sighed. "Is there anything else you can show us?" I asked Rich. "Because I have to admit, we don't have many credible leads right now."

Rich nodded slowly. "I could show you our interviews with the parents," he suggested, "but I should warn you, they're difficult to watch."

I looked at my brother. "We'll watch them," said Joe. I think he understood the look I was giving him.

We were down to the wire here. And we needed all the help we could get.

Rich was right about one thing: The interviews *were* hard to watch. And unfortunately, they didn't tell us anything we didn't already know. All of the parents—even Jacob—seemed understandably crushed by the loss of their child. There were lots and lots of tears, lots of *if onlys* and *I can't believes* and *I should have paid more attentions*. Of course all the parents were just beating themselves up. But I could imagine that after losing a child there was no way to accept that you couldn't have prevented it.

"Was it helpful?" Rich asked when he came back into his office after we'd watched all the videos. Joe was discreetly trying to wipe his eye, and I think we both looked wrecked.

"Not really," I admitted. "They all looked pretty crushed in their interviews."

Rich nodded. "They *were* all crushed," he said softly. "And I didn't know what to tell them. Truth be told, I still don't know what to tell Edie or Jacob."

I stood up, looking the detective in the eye. "Rich," I said, "do you really believe these all could have been bear attacks?"

He sighed, looking from the dark video screen to Joe and me and back again. "No," he said flatly. "But I don't know what they *were*, either. I haven't got any idea. In all my years in law enforcement, I have nothing to compare it to."

When we finished at the police station, since we were already in town, we decided to head over to the hospital. Rich ran us over and dropped us off.

"I don't feel any closer than we were this morning," Joe said with a sigh. "I can't imagine who would want to hurt all those kids. Or who would want us to stop researching it so badly that they'd try to scare us off."

I nodded. "It's frustrating," I agreed. "But maybe something will happen with Justin today that will get us a little closer."

Inside the hospital, we headed straight for the nurses' station on the psych floor. Chloe, the candy striper, was sitting at the desk chatting with Dr. Carrini.

"Oh, hello," she said with a big smile when she saw me walking up. "Good to see you boys again. But you should know that Justin's asleep right now."

I sighed. "Just our luck."

Chloe touched my arm. "Don't worry. He naps on and off all day. I'm sure he'll be up soon."

Joe glanced over at Dr. Carrini. "Any change since yesterday?"

The doctor shook his head. "I'm afraid not. I'm getting more concerned, to be honest with you. Chloe and I were just discussing the possibility that he may never recover his early memories."

I raised an eyebrow. "You really think that's possible?" I asked. "After spending five years with the Greers?"

Dr. Carrini straightened his spine. "It's extremely rare but certainly possible, especially considering the trauma Justin may have experienced. I mean, living in the woods for twelve years . . ."

I startled. "Wait a minute. You really think he lived in the woods for twelve years?"

Dr. Carrini looked surprised that I was challenging him.

"It just seems hard to believe," Joe explained, "that he would have lived so close to civilization for so long and never wandered into town."

"Or that he's so polite," I added. "He seems to understand social norms in a way that a kid raised in the woods, well, wouldn't."

Dr. Carrini glanced at Chloe, who nodded as if she knew what he was about to say. "It's unusual," he said finally, "but not entirely impossible. If he were truly disoriented by the bear attack—if he had trouble accessing his early memories even then—"

"He wouldn't have known to look for civilization," Chloe put in. "Because he wouldn't have known what civilization was!"

I frowned, looking from Chloe to the doctor. Was Chloe really buying this? I knew Dr. Carrini was the expert here, but I just couldn't believe that Justin had spent twelve years in the woods.

"What about the politeness?" I asked. "His

language skills are good, and he seems to understand what people expect from him."

Dr. Carrini nodded, looking thoughtful. "It *is* possible for young people to pick up on social cues very quickly," he said, "and perhaps—not definitely, but perhaps—he's accessing memories of language from his early years."

I glanced at Joe, knowing that I probably wasn't doing a great job of hiding my disbelief. What Dr. Carrini was suggesting . . . it just didn't add up.

Chloe seemed to sense my doubts and turned to me with a smile. "Justin is a very unusual case," she told me. "Dr. Carrini says he's never seen a case this difficult or surprising. It just seems like a lot of things that don't seem possible *could* be possible here. Otherwise how could Justin have gotten to this state?"

Joe didn't exactly look convinced, either. "Does Dr. Hubert think Justin might have been in the woods all this time?" he asked. I nodded, remembering the medical doctor we'd met when we were first introduced to Justin.

Dr. Carrini looked pained. "Not *exactly*," he admitted. "Dr. Hubert is very . . . old-school, I guess you might say." Suddenly he looked over my shoulder at someone approaching and smiled. "Mr. Greer! How are you this afternoon?"

I turned around. Sure enough, there was Jacob, stuffing a cell phone into his shirt pocket and looking a little uncomfortable. "Hello, doctor," he said, nodding at each of us. "Chloe. Boys."

"How are you this morning?" asked Chloe with a concerned look.

Jacob laughed uncomfortably. "Better," he admitted. "This hasn't been easy, but . . . well, maybe Edie's right. Justin might remember us at any time. We'd just better be patient."

Dr. Carrini nodded and gave a tight smile, even though this directly contradicted what he'd been telling us earlier. "Well, I'd better check on my other patients," he said and quickly disappeared down the hall.

"I should go, too," Chloe agreed, standing up. "See you later, Frank and Joe. And Jacob." Nodding at each of us, she took off down the hall.

Just then, there was a girlish squeal from down the hall. "Jacob!" a young female voice cried. And then a young woman came into view, perhaps in her midtwenties, with long auburn hair and a dazzling white smile. She ran down the hall toward Jacob and threw her arms around him. "It's so good to see you! I'm sorry I couldn't be here for you all week."

I glanced at my brother. *What the . . . ?*

But his focus was still on the woman, who was smiling at us now. "I'm sorry," she said, thrusting out her hand. "I don't mean to be rude. I'm Donna McCabe, Jacob's girlfriend."

Girlfriend? Jacob had a girlfriend? This was new information. Why had he never mentioned Donna before?

I didn't get much time to ponder this question, because within minutes of Donna's arrival Edie came running out of Justin's room like her feet were on fire. She was headed right for Jacob, and if she was surprised to see Donna, she didn't show it.

"Jacob, boys," she said, looking from her ex-husband to Joe and me. "Come quickly! Justin just woke up . . . and he remembers something!"

False Memories

A few minutes after Edie fetched us, a small army was gathered in Justin's room: Frank and me, Dr. Carrini, Dr. Hubert, Chloe, Edie, and Jacob. (Donna had excused herself to the cafeteria—she was worried about confusing Justin, since they'd never met.)

Before Justin could tell us what he told Edie, though, Dr. Carrini insisted on doing a quick exam. He checked Justin's pulse and blood pressure, and he shined a bright light in his eyes until Jacob couldn't take it anymore.

"Come *on*, doc!" Jacob cried, shaking his head in disbelief. "Why can't the boy just talk? You're makin' him forget what he was sayin' in the first place!"

Dr. Carrini pursed his lips and glanced at Jacob with disapproval. "I'm making sure Justin is lucid," he replied coolly. "I want to be certain he's aware of what he's saying and not producing false memories."

"*False* memories—," Jacob started to grumble, but Dr. Carrini cut him off.

"He appears to be fine," he said, backing away from Justin's bed. "Go ahead, Justin. Tell them what you remember."

Justin looked nervously at Jacob, then at Edie. Edie leaned over and took his hand, smiling encouragingly. "It's all right, Justin," she said softly. "Just tell them what you told me."

Justin cleared his throat and nodded. "Well . . . ," he said quietly in his scratchy, nearly-unused voice. "I remember a party."

Dr. Carrini nodded. "What sort of party, Justin?"

Justin stammered, "Well—I—"

Edie cut in gently, "What do you remember about the party?"

Justin nodded again. "Right. I remember big purple balloons and a cake that looked like a clown. And there was . . . there was . . . a big purple dinosaur there!"

Dr. Carrini scoffed. "Edie and Jacob, I think we can agree this—"

But Edie was smiling. "No, no," she said. "He's right! For his fifth birthday party, we had a Barney theme. And we had a man come dressed in a Barney costume!"

"He handed out the balloons," Justin added, speaking directly to Edie this time.

"That's right," Edie said, nodding and wiping a tear from her eye.

I turned to Dr. Carrini. This was pretty incredible! Justin's first memory of his early life in twelve years!

But oddly, Dr. Carrini looked perplexed. "Do you remember anyone there, Justin?" he asked brusquely. "Any of the guests?"

Justin glanced at Edie, and she squeezed his hand. "I remember you," he said to Edie. "You were wearing a blue dress. And you told me, 'Justin . . .'"

Edie began to tear up, and she wiped at her eye with her hand. "'Justin, you're our special baby. You were chosen for us, and we're so happy to have you.'"

Edie began to cry in earnest then, and Justin's eyes welled up, too. Chloe moved closer to the bed, grabbing tissues from the nightstand and handing them to both.

Everyone was quiet for a minute or two. Then Jacob's gruff voice split the silence.

"What about me, boy?" he asked, moving closer to Justin's bed. "You remember me?"

Justin looked up, startled, and shook his head.

"You sure?" Jacob asked. "I was there, you know. I set up the sprinkler for you kids to run through. I gave you a big monster truck you'd been wantin'. You don't remember?"

I swallowed. Jacob's naked desire to be acknowledged was hard to watch. But again, Justin shook his head without a word, then glanced down at the tissue in his hand. Jacob was silent, looking like he wanted to say more, but then he just huffed and backed away.

"Justin," I said, feeling a little awkward as I moved closer to the bed, "what about the night you disappeared? Do you remember anything about that?"

Dr. Carrini looked at me in alarm. "Maybe we should just pause here . . ."

But I wanted to hear what Justin had to say. "Do you remember going camping?" I prompted. "Sleeping in a tent with Edie and Jacob? Do you remember that?"

Justin looked troubled, like he was searching

inside his head and finding nothing. I was pretty sure he was going to say "no," when suddenly he said in a small voice, "I remember cooking hot dogs over the fire."

Edie gasped, then turned to Jacob with a look of amazement. "We did that!" she cried. "We did that, Justin, the night . . . well." She paused, probably not wanting to relive the difficult memory.

"Anything else?" Frank asked, stepping up behind me. "Justin, do you remember more from that night? Anything from the middle of the night?"

Justin squinched up his face. "Um . . . well . . ." He was clearly thinking hard. Finally he opened his eyes. "I remember . . . being outside?"

"At night?" Frank prompted. "You remember being outside in the dark?"

Justin opened his eyes and nodded. Then he closed them again, furrowing his brow. "I remember . . . a bright light?"

Dr. Carrini stood from the chair near Justin's bed he'd been perching on. "I think we should stop there," he said, in a tone that seemed to dare any of us to disagree.

"Stop?" asked Dr. Hubert. "But the boy is finally remembering."

Dr. Carrini frowned, placing a comforting hand on Justin's shoulder. Justin moved away, toward

Edie. "He's overexerting himself, clearly. And besides . . . the night of the camping trip is a police matter. Shouldn't Detective Cole be here?"

There was some grumbling, but most of us seemed to agree (albeit reluctantly) that yes, Rich probably should be there.

Dr. Carrini walked toward the door. "I'm going to get Justin a light sedative," he said, "to help him rest. And perhaps we all can leave Edie and Jacob here to have some one-on-one time with their son. We'll call Detective Cole and set a time to continue the questioning tomorrow."

I glanced at Frank, and he nodded. Slowly, everyone except Jacob and Edie filed out of the room.

We found ourselves in the hallway with the two doctors and Chloe. Once out of earshot, Dr. Hubert turned excitedly to Dr. Carrini. "He's remembering!" he exclaimed. "He's really remembering!"

Dr. Carrini smiled wryly. "Is he, though?" he asked.

"What does that mean?" asked Frank.

Dr. Carrini sighed. "I can't be sure, but I'm concerned that Justin is producing false memories."

I frowned. "Why would you think that? Edie confirmed the party memory."

"That's true," Dr. Carrini allowed, "but we weren't there when he first produced the memory. I'm afraid that Edie is so eager to be recognized, she might have inadvertently fed him information."

"How so?" asked Frank.

"For example," Chloe spoke up, glancing first at Dr. Carrini as though seeking his permission to explain this part. After he nodded, she went on. "Justin tells Edie, 'I remember a party.' A party is a very common occurrence in a child's life, so he might have been remembering his own party, or he might have been remembering one he saw on TV."

I nodded. "Okay. And?"

"Edie becomes excited," Chloe went on, "and gives Justin some nonverbal cues that he's on the right track. Smiling, nodding, that sort of thing. Then she says something along the lines of, 'What color balloons were there?' That tells him there were balloons, so he chooses a color. Perhaps he's right, or perhaps he chooses the wrong color but Edie corrects him—incorrectly interpreting that at least he remembered there were balloons."

I nodded. "Okay. But—"

Dr. Carrini held up his hand. "Then," he added, "the boy begins to focus on this false memory of a party with purple balloons. The more he thinks about it, the more he believes it really happened and that he was there. You boys might have experienced something similar at some time. Can you tell me about your first birthday party, for example?"

"Sure," I replied. "There were red balloons and a fire-engine cake. My aunt Trudy ate too much and got sick."

Dr. Carrini smiled. "Well, it might interest you to know that there's no way you could truly remember that. It's extremely rare for people to remember anything before the age of three—it's unheard of before the age of two. They call it infant amnesia."

I frowned. "Then why do I know the details?"

Chloe spoke up again. "You've probably seen pictures of the party your whole life, and your family has told you enough stories about what happened that you believe you remember," she explained. "But you don't *really* remember. You're just parroting what you've been told."

Frank was nodding slowly. "Interesting," he said. "And you think this is happening with Justin?"

Dr. Carrini sighed. "Look at what he's recalled so far. A birthday party with balloons. A camping trip with hot dogs. All very common scenes. Perhaps he's really recalling them, or perhaps—"

"He's just saying what people seem to want him to say," I finished.

It was a disappointing thought, but I had to admit, when Dr. Carrini explained it, it sounded possible. Although, the details Justin had produced for the Barney party—had Edie really planted those? Or was the memory real?

As I was pondering this, Jacob walked out of Justin's room and approached us with a sigh. We looked at him in surprise, and he simply said, "He don't remember me. Not much point in me being there. I'm gonna run into town for a coffee, cool off a bit."

Frank nodded, looking at me. "We should go too."

"You boys need a ride?" Jacob offered. I looked at my brother. Jacob had been a little unpredictable before, but he seemed to have calmed down now. Besides . . . there was no denying the emotional difficulty of what he was going through.

"Sure," Frank agreed. "That would be really nice of you."

We followed Jacob down to the main floor, chatting casually about the weather and how we'd been faring at the campsite.

"It's been . . . interesting," I said, not wanting

to get into details about the mystery man or the events of the last couple nights. "You know. It's beautiful out there."

Jacob nodded, leading us out of the building and toward the parking lot. "It *was* beautiful," he said quietly. "To me . . . I can't really see it that way anymore."

Of course. All at once, I remembered that Jacob had lost his *son* near our campsite, and I felt like a dope for calling it beautiful. What could you say to a parent who'd lost their child?

I didn't get much time to ponder that, though, because Jacob had stopped—in front of a huge black SUV.

"You boys can fight over who wants the front seat," he said, clicking open the doors and grabbing the driver side, "but I control the radio, okay?"

I grabbed Frank's arm right before he climbed into the passenger side.

"We can't get in this car!"

FRANK

10

Slashed

"**O**h, that's okay, actually, you know what, I think Frank and I are just going to walk around town," my brother started spouting as Jacob climbed into his SUV.

"What?" Jacob asked, climbing out and fixing Joe with an "are you crazy?" look. "I thought you boys were headed back to camp. Anyhow, I'm going into town for a coffee, so I can drop you there."

"That's okay!" Joe insisted, shooting me an urgent look. "We, uh, we need to . . ."

"We could use the walk," I filled in. "You know, we uh . . . we had a big lunch. And we need to run some errands in town, so we shouldn't hold you up."

Jacob was still looking at us like we were nuts, but he nodded slowly. "Well . . . all right." He nodded at us again and climbed back into his car.

A few minutes later, Joe and I were walking alone down the street toward town. "What was that about?" I asked.

Joe sighed. "Remember last night?" he asked. "The guy I chased through the woods to the road?"

That's when it clicked. "Oh, man—he was driving a black SUV, right?"

Joe nodded.

I frowned. "Do you think—you think it really could be Jacob who's trying to scare us? What would his motive be?"

Joe shrugged. "I don't know anything for sure. But if it *were* Jacob, he definitely knows we're there and looking into Justin's disappearance. Maybe he has something to hide. Maybe he wants to stop us from researching Justin's disappearance—no matter what he has to do to make us stop."

I thought this over. "Of course, he thinks we're only writing a paper. He doesn't know we're working with Rich."

Joe nodded. "But if he wanted to hide something badly enough, he'd want to stop *anyone* from learning about it—not just the police."

I sighed. "I don't know what to think anymore. Even if Jacob were involved in Justin's disappearance, would that tie him to the other kids?"

Joe shook his head. "I can't imagine he was involved in all the missing kids' cases. But maybe being involved in Justin's case would be enough for him to want us gone."

We were quiet for a while, silently trudging toward the town center.

"One thing's for sure," Joe said after a few minutes. "We've got to put a call in to ATAC and get some surveillance equipment."

"Surveillance equipment?" I asked. "For what?"

"If our mystery man follows form, tonight's the night we get *L-O-S*," Joe replied.

"And?" I prompted.

"Just one more night before we're *L-O-S-T*, and then who knows what happens." Joe stopped in his tracks, giving me a meaningful look. "Tonight's our last night to figure this out," he said, "if we don't want to get hurt."

A few hours later, Joe and I were back at our campsite with bags of ATAC-supplied surveillance cameras and sound recorders. We got right to work setting them up according to the ATAC-supplied audio instructions that we'd uploaded to our MP3 players. The instructions were pretty simple, actually, and once we had all of our electrical equipment plugged into the two outlets that serviced our campsite, we got so absorbed in the setup process that we were both startled by a familiar voice an hour or so later.

"What in tarnation is goin' on here?"

I turned around from the tree where I was setting up a video camera. "I . . . well." Farley was watching us with a bemused expression, and I glanced questioningly at my brother. I hadn't wanted to let on to anyone besides Rich the fact that we were having trouble at our campsite. We really weren't sure who the mystery man might be, so we didn't want to reveal that his scare tactics were working.

Joe gave me a defeated look, though. *No use hiding it now.* "We've had some . . . disturbances in the middle of the night," he admitted with a shrug. "We thought this equipment might tell us what we're dealing with."

Farley laughed. "Oh, that's rich, that really is," he said, smiling a not-entirely-unfriendly smile. "You think a bear is gonna be scared away by a video camera?"

"Maybe not *scared away*," I admitted. "But we can look at the footage in the morning and see who was here. It's that easy."

Farley nodded in an exaggerated way, still clearly amused by us. "In case it's that Nathan ghost, right?" he asked. "Come to eat your brains?"

When neither my brother nor I responded, Farley smiled again and held up his hands in a conciliatory gesture. "Never mind. It don't matter. That camera you're tryin' to put up, though, boy—you gotta move it. That tree's not going to support the weight of that thing."

Before I could reply, Farley had taken the camera from me and was looking around for a better spot. "Here, on top of this rock. You can fasten it to the tree trunk right next to it. Let me."

I glanced at Joe. We weren't really sure of Farley's intentions—so I wasn't entirely comfortable with him handling our equipment. He seemed to know what he was doing, though, so I kept a close eye on him, helping him where I could.

Within another ten minutes, we were all set up.

"There you go," Farley announced, admiring his handiwork. "All ready for *America's Funniest Middle of the Night Wildlife Home Videos*."

"Ha-ha," Joe replied dryly, but he wore a reluctant smile. "What brought you to our campsite today, Farley? Just feeling social?"

Farley shook his head. "As it happens, I was checkin' on you boys." His face turned serious and he went on. "Because a bear's been spotted just a mile or so upriver. Big grizzly bear—a male. I wanted to make sure you two were okay and warn you to be 'specially careful tonight." He glanced at the cameras. "I guess you boys were way ahead of me."

"A bear?" I asked. "Do you think he might head up here?"

Farley shrugged. "It's possible," he replied. "Just make sure you put up all your food tonight. And if you hear"—he scowled—"*noises* tonight, you just be cautious, okay? Don't go chargin' out there with your Proton Packs or whatever, ready to capture a ghost. Because you might just be angerin' a hungry bear."

Joe looked at me, confused. "Proton Packs?"

"I think it's something from the movie *Ghostbusters*," I stage-whispered back to him.

Farley nodded. "You'll have to forgive me," he said with a wry smile. "I'm a little behind on my movie references. Now if you'll excuse me, boys, I got a camp full of campers to warn." He walked a few steps away, then turned and nodded at the two of us. "Don't worry," he said. "I'll come back and check on you two in the morning."

With that, he turned and slowly disappeared into the woods, leaving Joe and me alone—or so we hoped.

That night was the worst yet. While Joe was on the first watch, a huge thunderstorm broke out. He didn't even have to wake me for my shift—an earsplitting crash of lightning did it for him. We huddled in the tent for a moment, listening to the woods gone wild around us.

"Anything weird?" I asked, a little afraid of how my brother might reply.

He sighed. "I can't be sure," he said finally. "I heard moaning—I could've sworn it was a human being. But more likely, it was just the wind through the trees."

I nodded. "Any footsteps?"

Joe shook his head. "Nothing like that—yet."

Joe crawled into his sleeping bag, and I picked up my flashlight and magazine, though I doubted I was going to be able to focus for long. I was sure Joe would be up tossing and turning, but after a few minutes, his breath turned even and slow, and I knew he was asleep. We were both probably still exhausted from the night before.

For a while there were just the sounds of the storm—thunder crashing, wind howling, and rain pounding down. I tried to hear the noises just for what they were, the sounds of nature, but it was hard not to hear voices in the wind or shouts in the crashes of thunder.

After about half an hour, a new sound started up that made my heart pound even harder. Sobbing— it sounded like a woman sobbing. First it came from the direction of the river, then it disappeared for a few minutes, then it started up behind me from the direction of the woods.

I struggled to hear the wind in the noise or something natural—the tail end of the thunder or a sound from the river. But I couldn't hear anything but the sounds of a woman crying.

I stood and, as quietly as I could, scooted over to the tent's door. As soon as I started unzipping the entrance, I heard another sound—our pots and pans, which we'd secured in the aluminum cooler. Someone was banging them together, trying to make noise!

I quickly unzipped the tent and, scared as I was, peered out into the slicing rain. But immediately, the noises stopped—all except for the wind and rain. I looked around our campsite, which was damp and windswept, but beyond that, nothing was out of place. Our fire pit was undisturbed. Our cooler was still closed, and nothing appeared to be out of place.

Getting wet, I zipped our tent back up and ran a hand through my damp hair. Breathing hard, waiting for my heartbeat to calm down, I picked up my magazine and flashlight. Within ten minutes, I heard the sobbing sound again, and the banging sound soon after. Each time I opened the tent to check outside, though, I saw nothing—and our campsite was just as we'd left it hours before.

As scientific and logical as I usually am, my mind wandered to the supposed Misty Falls ghost, Nathan. What else could make those noises but leave no signs? I knew there had to be another explanation, though. I *knew* it. Thank goodness we'd rigged up the surveillance equipment that afternoon—I couldn't wait to see what it showed.

Though I was sure there had to be some logical explanation, I was too tense and uncomfortable to relax during my whole shift. Sometimes the noises would come very close to the tent, like they were just feet away. I always stiffened, sure we were about to be invaded by some otherworldly being. Then the sounds would shift and move to the other side of the camp, yards from the tent. For hours, I tried in vain to get even a page read in my magazine.

When Joe's shift came around, I woke him eagerly. The storm had died down a bit, and the noises were less frequent. I was even beginning to wonder if I was imagining them now. Still, it was a huge relief to crawl back into my sleeping bag with Joe on the case. I didn't think there was any way I'd relax enough to fall asleep, but the next thing I knew, the sun woke me up.

Literally. I was woken by the sun shining right in my eyes. I squinted, trying to block the light with my hand, then turning onto my side. It was only after a few minutes that I realized the sun wasn't supposed to shine in our *tent*. I jumped up, turning toward the source of the light—and all the breath left my lungs.

Joe's sleeping bag lay there, empty.

And the sunlight was coming in through a hole someone had slashed in the tent right above his sleeping bag.

"JOE!!!!"

Good-byes

My brother came tearing out of the tent before I could even respond to his scream. *"Joe?"* he was shouting. "Joe! JOE!"

"I'm right here, Frank," I said, raising a hand from where I stood next to a fallen video camera. "Calm down. I'm sorry. I didn't mean to scare you by leaving the tent."

Frank looked at me, and all the tension in his face drained away. He sighed deeply, then shook his head. "What's going on?" he asked.

I gestured around to the cameras and recording equipment we'd so carefully set up the night before. "I guess the real question is, what happened last night?" I asked. "And the answer is, we'll never know."

"What do you mean?" asked Frank, coming closer.

"I mean we didn't get a single second of footage," I replied. "*All* of these cameras failed. The audio recording equipment, too. After that crazy night, we have nothing." I gestured to the ground in front of the tent. "Except that."

Scrawled in the dirt in front of the tent opening were the familiar letters: *LOS*.

Frank sighed again. "They were definitely here," he murmured. Suddenly seeming to remember something, he turned to face me. "What about the hole in the tent?" he asked. "Were you awake when that happened?"

I nodded. "That's what brought me back to the tent," I explained. "I was outside at the time, investigating a noise, when I heard a knife slashing through the tent fabric. I came running back."

Frank's eyes widened. "Did you see the guy?"

"No," I admitted with a sigh, "but I must have startled him enough to make him drop this."

I picked up a knife from the ground and held it out to Frank. It was a large hunting knife with a bone handle.

"I'm sure we can pass it on to Rich," I said,

"and he can test it for fingerprints or DNA or whatever . . ."

But Frank was shaking his head. "No," he said slowly, staring at the knife. Finally he looked up at me. "This looks familiar."

I was quiet for a minute, waiting for Frank to remember how he recognized the knife. He frowned, thinking hard, when suddenly I remembered . . .

"Farley!" I cried.

Frank nodded. "When he took us on the tour, the second site . . ."

I nodded, too. "He took out a knife and started cutting through the brush! It was a big hunting knife, just like this. And it had—"

Frank smiled. "A white handle. Just like this one."

I took a deep breath. "Wow. Do you really think . . . ?"

"And Farley helped us set up some of these last night," Frank pointed out, gesturing around to the cameras and recording devices. "Coincidentally, we didn't get any footage. Maybe . . ."

"Maybe he sabotaged them in some way?" I finished, thinking that over. "It's definitely possible. I tried to keep an eye on Farley yesterday, but if he knew what he was doing, he definitely could have done something to mess up the whole system."

"And if he's the guy trying to scare us," Frank added, "then he definitely has a motive for keeping us from getting any footage."

I nodded, sitting down on a big rock that jutted out toward the river. "Wow," I murmured. "Farley."

Frank moved closer. "He definitely knows all about the Nathan lore," he said, furrowing his brow. "He knows the park very well. He easily could have executed a plan to frighten us while we camped here."

"And all those stories about how dangerous the park is," I added. "He could have been trying to scare us then, too."

Just then, a shrill sound made both Frank and me jump. He turned toward the tent, then sprang into action. "That's my cell phone," he said, diving back into the tent to grab it.

A few seconds later he was back outside, the phone at his ear. "Oh, hello, Chloe," he said into the phone, his face turning a deep crimson.

I grinned. *Chloe?* She had his number?

Well . . . wasn't that *cute*?

Frank spoke quietly into the phone for a few minutes, then abruptly said, "I understand. Of course. If you can pick us up, we'll come right over."

After a quick good-bye, he hung up the phone and looked at me. "That was Chloe," he said, looking sheepish.

"I gathered," I said with a grin.

His expression turned serious. "She's coming to pick us up. She says things are pretty crazy at the hospital. Jacob left with Donna this morning on a flight out—complaining that he couldn't deal with this anymore. And Justin is really upset."

Start from the Beginning

"**W**hat happened?"

Joe and I arrived at the hospital about an hour after Chloe had called me, having been ferried over by Chloe herself. We stumbled upon Dr. Carrini, Dr. Hubert, and Rich, all standing in the hallway just out of earshot of Justin's room.

Rich looked up at us with a serious expression. "Jacob left this morning on a flight out," he explained. "He was acting stubborn and upset—I almost wonder if that girlfriend he had with him put some crazy ideas in his head." He sighed.

Dr. Carrini went on in a calmer voice, "He told us he 'just couldn't do this anymore' and he wanted to say good-bye to Justin. Unfortunately, his good-bye sounded a lot like an 'I'll never forgive you for not remembering me.' He talked a lot about feeling like a failure as a dad and not wanting to burden Justin with his inadequacies."

"Wow," breathed Joe, turning to me and shaking his head.

"Wow," I agreed. "How did Justin take it?"

"Not well," answered Dr. Hubert, who wore a concerned look on his gaunt face. "He became very upset once Jacob left. He began to cry. And then he told Chloe, who had brought his breakfast, that he remembered something about the night he disappeared."

I glanced at Chloe, who had given us the short version of this story in the car. "That's right," she agreed. "He was obviously feeling sad, and he took my hand and said, 'Chloe, I have something to tell everybody. I remember that night now. I *remember*.'" She paused. "So that's when I called you, and Detective Cole, too. I figured everyone would be interested in what Justin has to say about that night."

I nodded. "We sure are," I agreed. "Is Edie still here?"

Chloe nodded. "Yes, she and Hank have been in with Justin all morning, trying to soothe him. But

I don't know how successful they've been."

I glanced at Rich, who nodded. "Well, now that everyone's here, let's get started," he said, heading toward Justin's room. "I don't think it helps him at all to drag this out. Poor kid."

We all let out grunts of agreement, then followed Rich into Justin's room. Edie and Hank were sitting next to Justin's bed, and Edie was reading to him from an old-looking picture book. They both glanced up with what seemed like relief when we all walked in.

"Detective, boys, doctors," Hank said warmly. "Hello."

"Hi again, Hank," Joe replied, holding out a hand for Hank to shake. "Good to see you again. You too, Edie."

Edie nodded. "Justin has made a lot of progress this morning," she said like a proud mom. But then she added, "I think he's feeling confused and upset about Jacob."

Hank sighed deeply. "I can't believe he just left," he muttered.

I couldn't, either, but I didn't want to say anything to upset Justin further. Edie seemed to feel that way, too, because she shot Hank a "can it" look.

"Can we begin now?" asked Justin, sitting up

from his pillows. He looked sad but eager to get this meeting over with. Suddenly I realized how weird it must have been for him to have such a small crowd around whenever he wanted to tell his parents something. I felt a little wave of regret in my heart. More reason to want to solve this case quickly, then—to give Justin some semblance of the normal life he deserved.

"Of course," said Rich, pulling out a small recording device and pressing the "record" button. "Okay, Justin, tell me everything you've remembered this morning—starting from the beginning."

Justin frowned, but then the expression faded quickly as he began his story. "The birthday party I remembered the other day," he began. "The one with the purple balloons?"

I caught a skeptical glance passing between Dr. Carrini and Chloe, but Rich just nodded casually. "Yes, I recall."

"I remembered," Justin said, then paused and swallowed hard, "after." He stopped, glancing at his mother, who nodded encouragingly. "We had a game at the party—where you were supposed to wear a blindfold and then attach a tail . . ."

"It was Pin the Tail on Barney," Edie interrupted, patting Justin's arm gently. "Go on, honey."

"When it was my turn," Justin continued, "I

couldn't see anything, so I pushed the blindfold down a little with the back of my hand," he said. "But my father caught me." His voice broke. "He got angry at me for cheating at the game—*really* angry. He said a real man doesn't cheat. And he made me spend the rest of the party in my room while my friends kept playing."

Justin put his head down and swiped at his eyes with the back of his hand. I glanced at Edie, who nodded slowly, looking a little embarrassed.

"That's right," she said quietly. "I tried to tell him Justin was only five, not old enough to be a 'man' yet, but Jacob insisted that Justin wasn't too young to learn wrong from right."

I looked at my brother, who met my eye with a serious expression. I knew we were both thinking the same thing: Between this memory and the fact that he left this morning, was it possible Jacob still knew more about Justin's disappearance than he was letting on?

"Justin, son," Rich said in a husky, gentle voice, "I don't want to upset you, but can you tell me what you remember from the night you disappeared? The night you went camping?"

Justin looked up at him, and it was clear then that he was crying. Tears leaked from his wet eyes in little trails down his cheeks. But he nodded stoically. "Sure, um—"

"He doesn't remember the whole thing," Edie interrupted, looking at the detective with an expression that seemed to me to say "don't push him." "He just remembers waking up in the middle of the night, right Justin?"

Rich nodded. "Let's let him tell it. Justin?"

Justin took a deep breath. "I remember waking up in the middle of the night," he said. "It was dark, and I was scared because I wasn't in my room. But then my eyes adjusted, and I remembered we were in a tent, and that's when I saw him." He paused, swallowing.

"You saw him?" asked Rich, leaning in. "You saw whom, son?"

Justin shrugged. "I don't know," he admitted. "It was a man I'd never seen before. He was tall, and he had gray hair, and he was wearing a black shirt. And he knew my name. He said, 'Justin, I'm a friend of your parents', why don't you come out here and talk to me a minute?'" He paused, looking sheepishly at his mother. "So I did. I got out of the tent."

Rich nodded. "Then what happened?"

Justin closed his eyes. "It was dark at the campsite, but the man led me away from the tent and turned on a flashlight. He said, 'Justin, I know your daddy is hard on you, but he's not your real daddy. I know where your real daddy is, and I can take you there. You'll have a happy life. You'll have everything you want, and no one will ever yell at you.'" Justin paused and let out a sob. "I was scared, but he sounded so . . . so . . . I dunno . . ."

"You went," Edie said softly, squeezing his hand. "It's okay, Justin. You were five. You didn't know any better."

Justin nodded, sobbing harder now. "I went," he choked out. "And that's all I remember."

Rich caught my eye, and I could see that he was finding this just as hard to be a part of as I was. He sighed and went on. "Justin, do you remember *anything* after that, anything at all?"

Justin shook his head, still crying, but before he could respond, Dr. Carrini moved in and held up his hand. "Let's stop here," he said firmly. "I think we should have a quick chat in the hallway." He gestured to Dr. Hubert, Joe, Chloe, Rich, and me—we were all standing in a clump fanning back to the doorway. He walked out into the hall, and the five of us followed. My mind was already spinning with the information Justin had given us. I caught Joe's eye and could tell he was thinking the same thing.

Rich cleared his throat, pointing at Dr. Carrini. "What was that about?" he asked sharply. "I was close to getting real information about where Justin was taken after he was abducted."

Dr. Carrini laughed—a sharp sound in the quiet hallway. "*Real* information?" he asked. "Are you sure about that?"

"What does that mean?" Rich demanded.

Dr. Carrini sighed, glancing at Chloe, who nodded as though she already knew what he was going to say and agreed one hundred percent. "Have you ever heard of false memories?" he asked.

"What?" Rich asked, then scoffed. "Oh, you have to be kidding me! Those were *negative* memories! Why would anyone make those up?"

Dr. Carrini frowned, making clear that he was *not* kidding. "Justin has clearly bonded with Edie. Edie responds favorably whenever he remembers *anything*, and it serves to strengthen their bond. Don't you think—"

"No," Rich interrupted harshly, "I don't. Dr. Hubert, do you agree with what Dr. Carrini is saying?"

Dr. Hubert hesitated, stroking his chin. "It's certainly possible," he said slowly. "Do I think it's happening in this case? No, not necessarily. But Dr. Carrini is the expert."

At that moment, Hank poked his head out of Justin's room, looking at the six of us curiously— and not entirely happily. "What's going on out here?" he asked. "Edie and Justin are a mess. And why did you stop the questioning?"

Rich sighed loudly. "I'm closer than I've been on this case in twelve years," he muttered, shaking his head and glaring at Dr. Carrini. "And you just stopped me from solving it."

Dr. Carrini's eyes flashed with anger. "Didn't you notice that this memory of that night doesn't match the one he gave yesterday?" he demanded. "The bright light . . ."

Rich rolled his eyes. "Oh, come on, that was so vague . . ."

"And it could have been the flashlight," I spoke up. Everyone turned to me like they had forgotten Joe and I were there. I felt a little sheepish. "You know," I added, "the bright light. It could have been the flashlight the man turned on."

Everyone was quiet for a moment, thinking this over.

"I have a question," said Joe, giving me a meaningful look. "What does anybody here know about Farley O'Keefe?"

Rich looked up. "Farley?" he asked, clearly surprised. "Well, he's a little cranky sometimes, but overall he's harmless. Why . . ."

But he broke off, suddenly staring over at Hank. Hank looked stricken.

"What's up, Hank?" Joe asked gently. Hank shook his head, but he poked his head back into the room, calling, "Edie! Edie, come out here for a minute."

After a few seconds, Edie appeared at the door, looking surprised. "Can I help?" she asked. "Justin is very upset . . ."

Hank glanced at Rich and then back at Edie, a concerned look on his face. "Joe here was just asking about Farley O'Keefe."

I was expecting Edie to look confused, but instead she looked even more shocked and upset than Hank had. "What about Farley O'Keefe?" she asked carefully.

I cleared my throat. "We have some reason to believe he's been harassing us at our campsite over the last few nights," I said. "Nothing definitive. But I just wondered if you knew of any reason Farley might want to prevent us from looking into Justin's case, or any of the others."

Edie closed her eyes, then swallowed hard. She

opened her eyes and looked at Hank, who gently placed his hand on her shoulder. "Tell them," he said softly.

Edie looked from him to me, and then to Rich. "I'm so sorry," she said quietly, so quietly that I could barely hear her. "I didn't tell you before because I wanted to protect his privacy. But Farley O'Keefe is Justin's biological grandfather."

L-O-S-T

"*W*hat?" someone cried. It took me a minute to realize that the voice was my own. *Farley and Justin are related?* My mind was spinning. This just didn't make sense.

Rich cleared his throat. "Edie," he said slowly, like he was trying to control his voice, "could you elaborate?"

Edie nodded, glancing back at the room like she was concerned about Justin overhearing. Understanding her gesture, we all scooted a little farther down the hall. Then Edie replied quietly, "Of course. I'm sure this comes as a shock." She paused, sighed, and then continued.

"I grew up here in Misty Falls, and I lived here

my whole life until I was twenty-five. At that point, Jacob and I had been married for three years, and I desperately wanted children. Unfortunately, I wasn't able to have children of my own. Around this time, one of our good friends who was in the army was sent to Iraq to fight in Desert Storm. His wife, Hailey, was a close friend of mine—we shared everything, and she knew how much I wanted children." Edie paused to take a breath.

"Hailey's husband was Sean O'Keefe—Farley's son. As you know, he was killed in Desert Storm—just a few weeks after arriving in Iraq. Hailey was devastated. She thought Sean was the love of her life, and she couldn't imagine living without him." Edie sighed. "A week or so after his death Hailey learned she was pregnant with their child."

Rich coughed. "I remember Hailey O'Keefe," he said, seeming to think this through. "I never knew she had a child with Sean."

Edie nodded. "That's because Hailey was so deep in her own grief, she knew she couldn't handle raising a baby right then. It would be too hard for her. Since she knew how desperately Jacob and I wanted a child, she asked if I would consider adopting her baby. Of course my heart broke for her, but I knew we could help her in this one way: We could take her child and give him a good home." She fished a tissue from her pocket and dabbed at her eyes, which shone with tears.

Rich was nodding slowly. "You moved out of town around that time. Was that because . . . ?"

Edie nodded. "Hailey was so devastated, I knew she wouldn't be able to handle watching their son grow up. We moved to Boise, and we arranged for Hailey to stay with us until she delivered. When Justin was born, she kissed him once and then handed him over to us. She moved closer to her parents in Texas as soon as she was able. And I don't think she ever looked back."

Rich nodded again. "And Farley never knew of the child?"

Edie closed her eyes tightly, as though she were trying to hold herself together. "Hailey didn't tell him," she said quietly. "At least, not at the time. A couple years later, she remarried and had another child, and I think that made her realize just how strong the parent-child bond is. She wrote to Farley and admitted that she'd had a son with Sean and had given him to us to adopt."

I glanced at Frank. "And was he upset?" I asked. "Did he want access to the child that you weren't willing to give him, maybe?"

Edie shook her head. "Just the opposite," she replied, her voice low. "He sent us the most lovely note, just telling us that if we were so inclined, he would love to meet his grandson, but he understood if we felt uncomfortable. That's when they started," she said, looking at Rich again. "These yearly camping trips to Misty Falls Park."

Rich shook his head, as though he were trying to understand. "So Justin spent time with Farley on these trips? Did he know he was his grandfather?"

"No," said Edie. "I mean, yes, they spent time together. Farley taught Justin to read a compass and how to build a fire with just two sticks and a piece of flint. But as far as Justin knew, Farley was just the kindly park ranger. And Farley always seemed happy with that arrangement."

Frank looked confused. "What about Jacob?" he asked. "Did he and Farley get along?"

Edie pursed her lips. "They . . . tolerated each other. I don't think Jacob approved of Farley taking over his role, in some ways, and Farley made it clear that he didn't exactly think Jacob was father of the year."

"What does that mean?" Rich asked.

Edie sighed. "Farley thought Jacob should be more attentive to Justin. Jacob liked to do his own thing, read his book, go for hikes alone. And I think Farley thought that Jacob should be more of a mountain man, more like him—Jacob wasn't a huge fan of the outdoors. He couldn't read a compass or build a fire." She paused, then added softly, "You know how Farley can be."

Rich was nodding slowly. "This is all very interesting," he said, looking up at Frank and me.

"It fits," I spit out, before I could think better of it. "Farley's ranger uniform is dark, and he has gray hair. He knows the park better than anyone— he would know how to sneak up to the campsites and where to bring the kids so they wouldn't be found."

"And that stuff about a 'bad' daddy versus a 'real' daddy—that all makes sense if Farley disapproved of Jacob and knew he was Justin's biological grandfather," said Frank.

Rich looked as if he were still thinking it over too. "What about after Justin disappeared?" he asked, turning back to Edie. "What did Farley say then?"

Edie shrugged, then dabbed at her eyes again. "He told us how sorry he was, and I thought he was sincere," she said. "But he told me he truly thought Justin had been attacked by an animal. When the disappearances continued, he always upheld that they were animal attacks, not crimes. And he asked me to protect his privacy and avoid a scandal by not telling anyone about his relation to Justin." She paused, glancing apologetically at Rich. "That's why I felt it was okay not to tell you about his connection to Justin."

The detective blinked and nodded, as though he understood. He looked over at Dr. Carrini. "Still think those were false memories?" he asked, almost challengingly.

Dr. Carrini looked surprised, as though he didn't think we remembered he was there. But soon his expression turned to one of resignation. "I don't know what to think," he admitted slowly. "I can't say for certain either way. What you're saying certainly *seems* to make sense."

Rich nodded at Frank and me, then placed his hand on his holster and backed away. "If you'll excuse us, then," he said, glancing around at Edie, Hank, Chloe, and the two doctors. "I think we need to pay a visit to Farley O'Keefe."

That's when Edie began to sob in earnest.

Farley's log cabin in the forest looked almost disturbingly normal, considering what we now expected he could be involved in. His Jeep was parked in the driveway and a neatly manicured pathway led up to a green front door. I don't know what I was expecting—dungeons in the basement?

Kids being used for slave labor in the yard?—but this peaceful home was not it.

Rich led us to the front door and held up his hand to knock. When his knuckle hit the door, though, it gave way and swung open a few inches—it was unlocked, not even latched. He glanced at us, raising an eyebrow.

"Farley?" he called. "Farley, it's Rich—can we come in and talk to you?"

No answer.

Glancing back at us with a confused look, Rich pushed the door open all the way. The sound of a television hit us immediately—a talk show was playing at a normal volume. I glanced at my brother and shrugged. Odd to think of a mountain man like Farley settling down for an episode of *Maury*.

"Farley!" Rich called again. *"Farley!"*

Besides the television sounds, there was only silence.

Stepping into the living room, Rich frowned. "His Jeep's in the driveway," he said. "He can't have gone far."

Frank nodded. "Maybe he's off on a hike?"

I looked around. "Odd that he would leave the TV on," I observed. I was beginning to get a creepy feeling. Were we walking into a trap?

Rich sighed. "Well, let's take a quick look around. Maybe he's napping. He *is* getting older, and maybe his hearing's not what it used to be."

Maybe, I thought. But the creepy feeling still prickled at the back of my neck. If Farley really were involved in the disappearances of the Misty Falls Lost, that made him a pretty bad guy. And if he was willing to put in all that effort to freak out Frank and me at our campsite in the middle of the night, what might he be willing to do to us if we entered his home?

Even though we didn't exchange words, a quick look at Frank told me that he shared my concern. We stuck close to Rich as we slowly moved from room to room, Rich holding his gun at the ready, still calling, "Farley? Farley!"

The entire downstairs was clear, and a large window in the den was open, with the screen up.

"Do you think he escaped on foot?" Frank asked. "Could he have known we were coming?"

I nodded, thinking. "Maybe he realized he left his knife at the campsite this morning?"

Rich sighed. "If that's true, he could be any-where in the park right now," he said. "Farley would know all the nooks and crannies to hide in. And he could live in the wilderness pretty much indefinitely, with his skills."

That's when we heard a *clunk* from upstairs.

Rich glanced at us, then wordlessly nodded toward the stairs. He began climbing, and the two of us followed quietly. Upstairs, there were only two rooms—a guest bedroom, which was open and empty, and a closed door that led, I assumed, to Farley's bedroom.

Rich held out his gun, gestured to the two of us to hang back, and then put his hand on the door.

I swallowed hard. Was Farley in there?

It all happened in a flash. Rich pushed hard on the door and called, "*Police!* Farley, are you in there?" He aimed his gun into the room, but we were met by silence. The door faced another open window, but there were no human sounds inside.

Rich walked in, and Frank and I followed hot on his heels.

We only walked a few steps before Rich gasped and stopped short.

I followed his eyes and screamed.

There, on the bed, was Farley—or what remained of Farley. He was covered in blood, having been stabbed multiple times in the chest. A knife—I realized, after a moment, that it was bone-handled—lay on the floor. It was probably what we'd heard fall a few moments earlier. It must be Farley's own knife, which meant the knife our intruder had left wasn't his.

Blood soaked the white bedspread he lay on, and as my eye traveled up, I saw it:

L-O-S-T, scrawled in Farley's own blood, at the head of the bed.

Helpless

All right. So the culprit wasn't Farley. Or else, Farley *was* involved somehow, but so was someone else. Or, more likely, Farley knew something about the abductions that someone else wanted to keep secret, and *that* person was willing to murder Farley to keep him from sharing what he knew.

Whichever it was, we were now without suspects.

And our last night was coming on fast.

"Rich," I said quietly when he brought us to his car to drive us back to the campsite, "we're so sorry about Farley."

Farley's cabin was now swarming with police, and Rich looked exhausted and sad. I knew that they weren't best friends, but Misty Falls was a small town, and he had to be upset by the brutal murder of someone he'd known for years.

"Yeah," agreed Joe. "He was a little gruff with us, but generally he seemed like a nice guy. And it's too bad Justin had to lose his biological grandfather."

Rich was still for a minute, but then he nodded, catching Joe's eye in the rearview mirror. "I appreciate that," he said, "although I'm realizing there was a lot more to Farley than met the eye. Makes you wonder how well you really ever know your neighbors."

Joe and I nodded slowly, thinking that over, as Rich put the car in gear and pulled away from the crime scene.

"Rich," I said after a couple minutes had passed, "I don't want to take your attention away from Farley's murder, but I think something is going to happen at our campsite tonight, and we may have one last chance to find the person who's trying to scare us away."

Rich nodded. "I've thought about that," he agreed. "If the person harassing you is spelling *L-O-S-T*, and they almost certainly are, that means tonight is the last night."

Joe leaned forward. "Exactly."

"I'm going to guard you myself tonight, boys," Rich went on, "and I'm bringing another officer with me. After what happened today, I want to make sure you're kept safe at the park. And I agree with your thinking. This might be our final chance to catch someone who knows something about these disappearances, and about Farley's murder, too."

That night, our tent was a little crowded. Rich and his fellow officer, Kurt Donnelly, the twenty-something redhead we'd met on our first day, insisted on joining us inside the tent rather than give away to the mystery intruder that we were being guarded in any way. Even with the police in our tent, I had to admit, I was feeling nervous. It wasn't that I expected something to happen with the police there, exactly—it was that I didn't know *what* to expect. And that freaked me out a little. Okay, a lot.

Still, after we settled into our tent and turned off our flashlights, it was dead silent. Rich and Officer Donnelly had told Joe and me that we could sleep if we wanted—they would stay awake to guard the site—but I couldn't relax enough to drift off. After a few minutes, though, I heard Joe's breathing turn heavy and slow, and I knew he'd drifted off. My heart was pounding a mile a minute, though. I struggled to take even breaths.

It felt like endless hours ticked by, but it was probably only an hour or two. I didn't hear a thing other than the occasional sigh or throat-clearing from Rich and Officer Donnelly. I was beginning to wonder—what if this was all meant to psych us out? What if our mystery intruder never intended to come back tonight? Or maybe he'd heard about Farley, or he was *responsible* for Farley (that thought made me shiver), and he decided to take the night off?

It must have been around one or two in the morning when I heard it. A slow shuffling sound, like a big man dragging himself through the woods. It was far away at first, several yards into the trees. But it got closer.

And closer.

And closer.

I felt my heart speed up, just as Rich turned on a small flashlight and looked from me to Officer Donnelly. His expression was serious; he heard it too.

The sound was just feet away from the tent

now; there was definitely someone out there. Rich, Officer Donnelly, and I sprang to our feet. As Rich was unzipping the tent and we were all peeking out, I heard it: a low, menacing, angry growl.

At that point, several things happened at once. As Rich, Officer Donnelly, and I crawled out of the tent, I heard Joe wake up and ask, "What's going on?" But at that moment, Officer Donnelly screamed, and I launched myself to my feet to see what was up.

And oh, my gosh. It was right there—just feet away. As I struggled to swallow my scream, the smell hit me.

Just an arm's length away from me was a giant grizzly bear!

It growled again, clearly having designs on me for dinner, and I sprang backward faster than I ever have in my life. For the next few seconds I was aware only of running and gasping for air, but then I heard the chaos I'd left behind me. The bear had turned away from me—thank God—and was headed toward Rich, who had tripped over a log near the fire pit and was struggling to get up. Behind the tent, Officer Donnelly was screaming again. Just then, I saw my brother poke his head out of the tent and realize what was going on. His eyes widened in alarm, and right at that moment a rock came sailing from Officer Donnelly from directly behind the tent, and it hit the bear squarely over its left eye.

The bear let out a furious bellow, turning toward the tent and my brother. My heart pounded in my chest and I opened my mouth to scream, but no sound came out. Officer Donnelly must have panicked; even Joe and I knew not to throw anything at an angry bear. Now the bear was advancing on my brother, and Joe was trapped by the tent—there weren't many places for him to go.

"Joe!" Rich screamed. "Run! Run *now*!"

My brother seemed to spring to life as the bear suddenly lurched forward and swung an angry claw in Joe's direction. He wasn't fast enough, though—the bear swiped him hard along his shoulder, leaving a nasty wound. Joe darted back into the tent then, pushing against the fabric of the walls so hard that the tent uprooted from the ground. I could see the outline of my brother's hands from inside the tent, scrabbling for the place where our earlier attacker had slashed it with the knife, trying to find a way to escape.

Just then there was a mighty shot, then another, and suddenly the bear swayed on its feet and fell forward, toward the fire pit. I turned and saw Rich holding a tranquilizer gun. He must have managed to get it from the stainless steel cooler where he and Officer Donnelly had stored extra supplies. For a moment, there was silence.

We'd been attacked by a real bear.

And we'd won!

I sprang into action, running toward the tent and my brother. Scrambling around the huge, unconscious bear, I grabbed the zipper opening and pulled it open. Joe was sitting inside, cradling his shoulder in his other arm. He looked pale, and he was bleeding a lot—but he was going to be okay. It was clearly just a flesh wound.

"Joe," I breathed.

"I'm okay, Frank," he said quietly, shaking his head. "That was pretty gnarly, though."

I chuckled softly. "Yeah, I guess Farley was right," I said, remembering his warning that a bear had been spotted in the area.

"He was right *tonight*," Joe corrected me, "but I think we're way beyond all of this being the work of some bear."

Everyone agreed that Joe was going to be all right, but Rich insisted on taking him to the hospital to be cleaned up and given antibiotics. He left me with Officer Donnelly, who was still apologizing profusely for throwing the rock.

"I should have known better," he admitted, shaking his head. "I just panicked when I saw it go after Rich . . ."

"Don't worry about it," I told him, settling back into the tent. "I freaked out pretty badly when I saw it going after Joe, too. I would have done about anything to distract that bear."

Officer Donnelly nodded and sighed. "That was awfully scary," he admitted.

It sure was. Joe and I had been exposed to a lot of freaky things in our work for ATAC, but that was about the closest I'd ever been to being mauled by a wild animal—or worse, to watching it maul my brother.

"You can get some sleep if you want," Officer Donnelly offered. "I'll stay up and take the first watch."

"Thanks," I said, dutifully climbing into my sleeping bag. Bear notwithstanding, we still thought our intruder might show up again tonight. I settled down on my pillow, but I seriously doubted I'd be able to fall asleep after all the excitement we'd just experienced, and who knew what excitement was still to come?

The next thing I knew, though, my eyes were fluttering open. I didn't know what time it was, but it had to be hours later. It was still dark outside. I heard footsteps near the tent, and I sprang up from my sleeping bag. As my eyes adjusted to the darkness, I realized I was alone in the tent. Officer Donnelly's hat and badge were lying on the floor and the tent opening was unzipped, flapping in the breeze.

An uneasy feeling washed over me. Was that Officer Donnelly I'd heard outside? If it was— why had he left his hat and badge inside?

I blinked, my mind still fuzzy from sleep. I heard a noise again, and crept toward the tent opening— I had to check this out. I had to push myself into action.

Outside, it was dark. I took my flashlight with me, but I wanted to avoid turning it on. Something told me that if it *wasn't* Officer Donnelly I was hearing—if it were something much worse— then I didn't want to announce my presence.

I waited a moment for my eyes to adjust further, then looked around the campsite. I didn't see anything out of the ordinary. Before he'd left with Joe, Rich had called the park's animal-control officer, and a team had come and taken the bear away on a truck to transport him closer to his known habitat. There were still prints and marks from where the bear had fallen, but otherwise, the campsite looked as it always had.

I walked toward the river and looked out over it, then to the right and left. Nothing unusual, just the soft gush of water flowing and the dancing of moonlight on the water. That left the woods. I took a deep breath and walked through the campsite toward them.

The woods, too, were quiet. I walked slowly around the perimeter of the campsite, still not seeing anything unusual—or any sign of Officer Donnelly. I tried to squint into the woods, but it was too dark to see much beyond a few feet. I bit my lip.

Then I took another deep breath and entered the woods.

It was quiet inside—quiet except for the hoot of an owl and the soft rush of the wind through the trees. I walked in about ten yards, then paused and listened. Wind, trees—all normal sounds. Maybe I should check the latrine area? Maybe Officer Donnelly was just quietly answering the call of Mother Nature?

I turned back toward the tent and had gone only a couple feet when I tripped over something. I pitched forward but caught myself before I completely lost my balance. I looked down at the ground and gasped, my heart jumping into my throat.

I turned on my flashlight.

I had tripped over the body of Officer Donnelly. He was lying facedown on the ground. He was wearing his holster, but it was empty. I put my hand on his back and could feel that he was still breathing, but very slowly—like he'd been drugged or was in a deep sleep.

Then suddenly, I felt a blow to the back of my head, and all I could feel was a throbbing, burning pain.

I pitched forward, falling onto Officer Donnelly now. He didn't stir, and I struggled to hold on to consciousness. Darkness invaded the edges of my vision, threatening to take me under. I used every ounce of energy I had to twist around and face my attacker.

A large, black-clad figure in a ski mask was looking down at me.

"You're a little old for my collection," he said in a husky smoker's voice. "But you'll do."

I saw him raise Officer Donnelly's gun over his head. I watched it come down, feeling helpless, unable to move. And then it made contact with my skull. My head exploded in pain again, and everything turned inky black and silent.

Taken

As it turns out, getting swiped at by an angry bear is more of a nuisance than anything else. I wasn't in a lot of pain from my wounds, which were mostly scratches along my shoulder, a few of them deep. But since I was bleeding, and since the bear likely had not had all his shots up to date, I spent a good long time in the emergency room. In fact, the sun had long since risen by the time Rich met me in the lobby, all bandaged and cleaned up. I squinted at the light streaming in through the windows and walked over to the detective with a sigh.

"All better?" Rich asked me, a smile playing at the corners of his lips.

"Better as I'm going to get," I confirmed. "But you should see the other guy!"

Rich chuckled, and together we walked out to the parking lot and climbed into his car.

"Any news from Frank or Officer Donnelly?" I asked.

Rich shook his head. "Not a peep," he replied. "And Officer Donnelly's not the type to hesitate to ask for backup, so I'm guessing it was a quiet night."

A quiet night. I sighed, thinking that over, as we drove through the town and into the park. A quiet night was a good thing, of course—it meant my brother was fine and healthy and hopefully even well-rested. But it was bad, too, in a way. It meant we weren't any closer to solving this case. And Farley was dead, and who knew what else the murderer was capable of?

Our only hope, I guessed, was that Justin would remember more as the days wore on.

A few minutes later, we were pulling into the parking lot about a mile from our campsite. Rich parked, and I heaved myself out of the car with a grimace.

"Does it hurt?" asked Rich, looking at my bandaged shoulder with concern. "Will you be able to hike to the campsite?"

I nodded. "I'm fine. It's just a little sore." I tried to look tough. "I've felt worse." Which was true, by the way. Working for ATAC isn't always a walk in the park.

We walked slowly down the trail to our campsite, listening for . . . well, anything unusual, I suppose. But all I heard was the cheeping of birds and the occasional scuttering of small animals along the forest floor. It was still early, and I knew much of the wildlife would be sleeping off a night of foraging for food. Including, I supposed, the bear that attacked me. I just hoped he was sleeping it off somewhere far, far away.

When we reached the site, we were greeted by silence. Rich smirked at me. "Just like I thought," he said. "They're probably catching up on their shut-eye, now the sun's up."

I smiled. I sure *hoped* Frank was getting some sleep after the week we'd had. Our tent hadn't exactly been a haven of relaxation and peace.

But when we stepped closer to the campsite, I could sense that something was wrong. The tent was still standing, but it seemed to list to the side. And as I sped up, running closer, I realized that our stuff was out of the tent and strewn all around the site. Our sleeping bags, pillows, clothes, books . . . everything had been disturbed, maybe even searched!

"Frank!" I called, instinctively worried for my brother. *"Frank!"*

But there was no answer.

Rich came running up behind me, his expression darkening as he took in the ransacked tent. "Oh, brother," he muttered, looking from the half-deflated tent to our bedding and clothes, which had been trampled by someone's muddy footsteps. "Frank!" he called, turning to the woods and raising his voice. "*Kurt!* Where are you?"

I took off then, unable to keep still. I ran to the river and looked left and right, but I didn't see any sign of Frank or Officer Donnelly. Then I turned around and looked at the woods. The sun was hitting them at an angle, so they looked gloomy and dark—darker than the rest of the park. I felt my heart speed up. When I had chased the mysterious black-clad figure out of our campsite, he had run through the woods.

Glancing at Rich, who was on his knees, looking into the tent, I gestured toward the trees. "I'm heading in there," I said.

Rich nodded and got to his feet. "Don't go alone. Not now. Let me follow you."

So I walked slowly toward the woods, Rich close on my heels. It was darker inside, and it took my eyes a moment to adjust. When they did, I looked around—and gasped.

Behind me, Rich cried out. "Kurt!"

It was Officer Donnelly—lying facedown in the mud.

Rich scrambled to kneel on the ground. He rolled the officer over and held his ear against his friend's mud-covered face. "He's breathing," he said. "But very slowly. I think he's been drugged."

I nodded, swallowing hard. *Drugged.*

As if someone had needed him out of the way.

As though someone couldn't let him witness what was about to happen . . .

To Frank.

My heart was pounding so hard I could barely hear anything else. I could feel adrenaline rushing through my veins, making me tense and edgy. Without another word to Rich, I ran farther into the woods, screaming, *"Frank! FRANK!"*

But there was no answer, no response at all. Finally I stumbled to a stop. I glanced back at Rich, who was watching me with sympathy.

I didn't say anything. I didn't have to. Slowly, afraid of what I might find, I walked back to the tent and forced myself to look at the ground in front of the entrance. I knew what would be written there before I saw it, but the letters still drove my heart up into my throat.

L-O-S-T.

My brother had been taken.